BEAUTY, BRAIN AND CHARACTER BBC

TWO DIFFERENT WORLDS {BOOK ONE}

By

LATEEFAH ADEWUNMI JUMAH

TABLE OF CONTENTS

ACKNOWLEDGMENTS 3

FOREWORD 7

CHAPTER ONE 10

CHAPTER TWO 19

CHAPTER THREE 28

CHAPTER FOUR 41

CHAPTER FIVE 48

CHAPTER SIX 54

CHAPTER SEVEN 64

CHAPTER EIGHT 74

CHAPTER NINE 85

CHAPTER TEN 98

CHAPTER ELEVEN 106

CHAPTER TWELVE 120

CHAPTER THIRTEEN 127

GLOSSARY 137

REFERENCES 139

ACKNOWLEDGMENTS

I give thanks to Allah who has made it possible for this vision to become a reality. My gratitude to Allah is immense. *Alhamdulillah RabilAlamin. Shukran Ya Rabb. Olohun modupe o.* My joy knows no bounds because my Lord has done me a huge favour; the favour of the realisation of this project. For this, I'm forever grateful to my maker.

To my husband, *iro mi to n jo, onilu e wanisale omi:* This means that my husband is my pillar of support. If support is a human, that'll be my lovely husband. He's ever ready to support me financially, morally, physically and emotionally. If I count my blessings, which of course is not possible, I'd count my husband uncountable times. I pray Allah enlarges you in every way. May you never be unfortunate. May the blessings, protection and favours of Allah be with you forever. Thank you sweetheart for being a shoulder that erects my neck.

My lovely children are super-duper amazing. They understand that mum is a writer and gives me serenity every time I need one. May Allah bless you for me. My siblings have been very supportive, may Allah reward you all with goodness. My lovely parents, your prayers have been doing wonders in my life. May Allah bless you both with goodness in both worlds.

I appreciate my sweet sis, Zulikha Jumah; umm Anas, for taking her time to proofread book 3, 4, 5, and 6. May Allah bless you extraordinarily, sweetheart. May He grant all your heart desires, Amin.

My profound gratitude goes to Mrs Lawal Risqah Omolola: LRO. This woman is the perfect definition of sweetness. She read BBC series from book 1-6 and her beautiful and honest reviews were what kept me going till the final stage. May Allah always make you happy.

She is always ready to listen to me and offer advice and her expertise free of charge. She's a grammarian par excellence. Whenever I need clarity on English grammar, I'll just go to her and I'll be attended to politely. May Allah never leave you to yourself even for the blinking of an eye.

My heartfelt appreciation also goes to Umm Abdirrahman Kifaayah Bukky. I can't even describe how awesome she is. My ustadha extraordinaire. Whenever I need clarity on Islamic matters, she's just a call away and she'll delight me with her proficiency which she's ever ready to lend free of charge. May Allah bless her beyond human comprehension. Through her, I met my awesome editors, Mrs. Bilqees Hambali, Mr. Olapade and Mr. Obasa, thank you all for the efforts you put in the book. I'm grateful.

Every name that appears on this series is imaginative except Mrs. Abisoye and Miss Adeola. Mrs. Abisoye, as used in this book, was my IRK teacher in high school; Anwar-ul-Islam Girls High School, Ojokoro, Ahmadiyya, Lagos. This is to honour her. She was such a dutiful and highly impactful teacher, may Allah bless her wherever she is, *Aamin*. Whenever I see a dutiful teacher, I see Mrs. Abisoye, *Awwwwww*, I loved her so much. Students needed not remind her of her lessons. She was always punctual and unfailing. Miss Adeola on the other hand was my Biology teacher in the same school. She was an embodiment of sweetness. Oh my God! Miss. Adeola has a large heart, a really large one. Her heart was large enough to accommodate her students in the school and outside the school. Her home became our second home. Very hospitable and warm. She shared her food with us. She shared her clothes with us. She was generous with her money. She kept up with our growth till we got married, how amazing!!! Oh my goodness! I'm short of the right words to describe this beautiful soul. May Allah bless her immensely and shower His mercies upon her children. Using her name as an impactful teacher in this series is to honour her in my own little way. May Allah honour her beyond human comprehension, *Aamin.* Watch out for the impactful Miss Adeola in book 5 and 6.

Another great woman that my pen must not fail to write about is Alhaja Ogundiran. She's one of the people that actually triggered my pen to compile this series but sadly. Alhaja Ogundiran was the former Ameerah of Fomwan, Oyo State chapter and she has been my no 1 elderly and supportive fan over the years. May Allah continue to shower His blessings on her, *Aamin.*

I have amazing people in my circle. One of such amazing people is Mrs. Munirat Shittu Motunrayo. The most cheerful human I've ever seen. Motivator par excellence. Since the day she read book 1 and 2, she's been on my neck to publish the books. She certified the books as a parent. Her words of encouragement were a positive push for me. May Allah continue to bless and honour you immensely.

To sister Mutiah Adesanya, thank you sis for being a darling. May Allah reward your kindness. My gratitude is not complete without appreciating the effort of Imam Sanni Kay Yusuf on this series. May Allah bless you immensely, sir.

My publisher, bro Suara Abiodun Isa, your zeal towards what you do is second to none. I appreciate your effort. May Allah crown your endeavours with unlimited success.

To high school students, these books, from 1-6 are dedicated to you. May Allah guide your steps to righteousness. May you be the coolness of your parents eyes. Aamin.

To parents, may you reap the fruits of your labour on these precious sprouts. Thank you all as you dip your fingers in your pocket to buy these books. May Allah replenish your pocket.

To schools, I'm sending my appreciation already because I'm hopeful of your support. May Allah bless you all.

To all my laj fingers supporters over the years, thanks for the trust you have in me. And for your love, I do not take it for granted. May you be rewarded in manifolds.

LATEEFAH ADEWUNMI JUMAH: LAJFINGERS
1443 AH - 2022

FOREWORD

It's a great honour getting to write the foreword for this all-encompassing, intriguing, captivating and knowledge filled book.

If you have been a fan of Laj Fingers Stories, you would agree with me that she isn't a mediocre writer; she is a prolific writer who gives her all into her stories. She is a talented writer with several good books to her record and I have read a reasonable number of them because I am a fan of good books myself. She writes brilliantly well, her fingers are indeed large.

She is a lover of young children and this explains why she came up with the idea of BBC.

Coming back to BBC, the story touches different aspects of life, religion, family, adolescence, friendship, rivalry, jealousy and a whole lot.

It explores some secondary school students; you will get to meet Adam, an intelligent young boy from a humble background.

Khadijah, a pretty and brilliant girl who has all the love, money, time and attention; she is from a wealthy home and the apple of her parent's eyes. Adam however happens to be a threat to her, Khadijah feels she deserves the best and no one else does. Adam wouldn't back down either.

Habeebah, a young girl who is left to hawk for her poor grandmother before they could feed, she is equally a brilliant girl despite her poor family background. Children from broken homes face a tonne of challenges. Habeebah is a product of one. Even though the vacuum left by her parents' separation affected her, she was still able to sail through with guidance from her good teachers.

You can achieve your dreams irrespective of your family background. Being born into a poor family doesn't mean your dreams are not valid. They are valid and would come to reality.

You will also get to meet Abass, the comedian who entertains everyone.

BBC talks about the different stages of adolescence and its challenges. It takes young children on sex education in the most decent manner you have ever come across in any book. Laj Fingers is a conscious Muslim and this reflects also in her writings.

Remember, children know more than we think they do and we need to catch them young and give them the right education as regards growing up.

BBC is a six series book, they are all designed in a way that suits each age bracket. Although it is in a series, each story is complete on its own. So, you don't have to worry.

I would love every parent to read this book because there is so much to learn even as a parent. There are quite a number of parental hacks in it. Parents need to understand the psychology of an adolescent child. This set of children needs all the love, attention and listening ears. Adolescent age can be overwhelming. BBC lets you know your adolescent child is not acting weird; it's a normal feeling even though caution is required.

I recommend BBC to every Muslim secondary school.

May Allah ease parenting for us and make our children sail through in this life and in the life to come.

Sit back and enjoy BBC!

LAWAL RISQAH OMOLOLA

A graduate of Mass Communication; a creative writer and a passionate teacher who makes learning fun and interesting.

She is popularly referred to as Iya Ajoke in cyberspace. She is the brain behind 'Ajoke Series' on Facebook, a page that is dedicated to English literacy, creativity development, content creation and lots more. She does this with style, I bet you wouldn't see this elsewhere!

CHAPTER ONE

The long holiday after the National Common Entrance Examination had finally come to an end. The new JSS1 students were getting ready for school resumption.

Kings and Queens College was a federal government school which had been in existence since 1990. The school was among the best federal schools in Nigeria, if not the best. With years of unfaltering academic excellence, a conducive learning environment which housed beautiful and well ventilated classrooms and highly experienced teachers, the school stood out among other federal schools.

Kings and Queens College had always witnessed a huge number of students picking the school as first and second choices. The school was that superb. Parents always wished their wards attended the school because of its consistent excellent academic records since the establishment of the school.

Apart from the brilliant academic records which the school had maintained so far, there were also other side attractions which captivated parents, as well as students. The good image of the school reflected on the graduates long after they left the school. The kind of respect the alumnus got whenever they mentioned Kings and Queens College as their Alma-Mater, was always exhilarating.

Due to the amazing and positive reviews by parents, students and alumni of the school, admission into the school was always a survival of the fittest. Due to the large entrance of students every year, the cut-off mark for admission increased. This consequently meant that only students who performed extraordinarily well in the National Common Entrance Examination could make it to the school.

Before the admission of any student into the school, such students must have initially passed the federal government cut-off mark before being qualified to take the entrance examination of the school. Thereafter, only students who excelled in the school's entrance examination were given admission. The school was often referred to as a school for the gifted.

The year's entrance examination of the school had been conducted during the long vacation. Students who triumphed in the examination had been given admission. They were only waiting for the resumption.

***

On the morning of the resumption day, Khadijah Oniru had woken up at 4:00 a.m. She was only 9, but waking up by herself had been her custom. She was tall and fair in complexion. She looked so much like her mother; pretty and stunning. Khadijah was characterised by wisdom and uprightness.

She was a highly intelligent girl who'd been independent of her parents for a long time. She was both independent in thoughts and actions that she needed not be told anything before she did it, especially when it had to do with her studies and caring for her body. The only thing she wasn't exposed to was house chores. And that was because there were tons of maids in her house available to do the chores.

She was so excited to go to school. She'd been eagerly looking forward to resumption since the day she passed Kings and Queens College's entrance examination. She didn't only pass the examination but also had the highest score.

Throughout her primary school education, she'd always maintained the first position. And it came as no surprise to her and her parents that she carried the exceptional performance on to secondary school.

Khadijah couldn't sleep well due to the excitement and longing of being a secondary school student. She couldn't wait to explore secondary school life for she had heard a lot of beautiful things about Kings and Queens College.

During the holiday, her parents had got everything she would need in school for her; some school shoes, a new fancy school bag and a beautiful lunch bag to match with it. She also got sets of inner-wears, pairs of white socks, a food flask and a host of other important things. Her parents got her more than enough, for money wasn't a problem - they were extremely rich.

After Khadijah opened her eyes at 4:00 a.m, she realised she had woken up quite early. She got out of bed nonetheless and went straight to the bathroom. She had a warm bath, dried her body with a towel and walked out of the bathroom. A glance at the wall clock in her room revealed it was only 4:20 a.m. She shrugged indifferently.

She didn't go back to sleep because that would ruin the bath she'd already had. After opening her wardrobe and bringing out her school uniform, she smiled at the sight of the uniform. She had an adrenaline rush at the thought that she was already in secondary school. Her school uniform and other necessary school items like textbooks, had been purchased during the holiday. She wore her uniform, a white shirt and green striped pinafore. She walked to the standing mirror in her room and tilted her green beret to the right side in front of the mirror. The image that stared back at her in the mirror made her smile; the uniform fitted her perfectly. She looked so beautiful in it. She smiled non-stop. She was more than ready for school.

By the time she finished dressing up, it was 5 minutes before 5:00 a.m.

After she heard the first *adhan* from the nearest mosque, she walked into the bathroom and performed ablution. She prayed two *rakats* and remained seated on the prayer mat.

At about 5:20 a.m, the second *adhan* was called by the *Muadhin* and she got up to pray *rakatain* fajr. She remained on her mat until she heard the *iqamah* for *salatul subh*. She prayed *subh* and headed downstairs when it was already 5:40 a.m. On her way to the living room, she met a maid and greeted her with smiles. The maid teased her.

"You're very early today, Khadijah. Is it because it's going to be your first day in secondary school?" The maid teased her.

"I've always been an early bird," Khadijah replied with smiles.

"Yes, that's true. You've always been an early bird. It's just that you are much earlier today," the maid remarked, while winking at her. She smiled and sat on the dining table.

"Should I serve your breakfast?" The maid asked.

Khadijah glanced at her glamorous wrist-watch which indicated 5:45 a.m before responding.

"Breakfast is ready, already?" Khadijah marvelled.

"Yes, madam instructed the cook to make breakfast earlier because it's going to be your first day in secondary school," the maid explained.

"I see. Please pack the food in my school lunch bag. I'll have cereal for breakfast," Khadijah replied.

"Alright, I will do that," the maid replied and went away.

Khadijah took some cereal and waited patiently for her parents to come out of their bedroom. Her parents do not come out of their room until 6:50 a.m during weekdays. They even stay in their bedroom till 8:00 a.m on weekends because they do not have to go to work. She hoped her mother would come out of her bedroom earlier that day because of her resumption.

Despite the fact that the family had two drivers, her mother had been her driver since she started kindergarten up till this moment. That responsibility was intentionally shouldered by her because she couldn't trust her daughter with a male driver.

Mrs. Oniru allowed the driver to take the boys to school. But she vested herself the responsibility of taking her only daughter to school, after which she would proceed to her office. She would also be the one to pick her from school. She had three of them; two boys, Abdullah and Haarith before Khadijah, who was the last child.

Abdullah and Haarith were both in secondary school. Their parents raised them to be as busy as bees. They were hardly ever at home. After school closed every day, they went for extra coaching in the home of their teacher. The extra coaching would last till 6:30 p.m. The driver would pick them from there. They always got home at the call to *maghrib* prayer.

They would observe *maghrib*, after which they would eat dinner with the rest of the family. During weekdays, the driver would take them to the *madrasah* where they would stay for the weekend and return home after school on Monday. That was how Chief and Mrs. Oniru raised their male children; to be as busy as a bee so that they would grow to be so industrious and live impactful lives.

Khadijah checked the time for the umpteenth time. The time was 6:55 a.m already and her mother hadn't come out of her room. "This is very unusual of her," Khadijah thought. She got up and headed towards her mum's room. On getting to the door, she grabbed the door handle to open the door, but quickly paused as she remembered the Qur'an verse she was taught by her home Quran teacher; *surah Noor* verse 58, which says:

"O ye who believe! let those whom your right hands possess, and the (children) among you who have not come of age ask your

permission (before they come to your presence), on three occasions; before morning prayer; the while ye doff your clothes for the noonday heat; and after the late-night prayer; these are your three times of undress; outside those times, it is not wrong for you or for them to move about attending to each other; Thus does Allah make clear the signs to you; for Allah is full of knowledge and wisdom."

She knocked on the door after remembering the verse. When she got no response, she knocked for the second time before her mother came out of the room. She greeted her mother with a long face and Mrs. Oniru realised she'd hurt her daughter by being late.

"Oh! I'm sorry, darling. I'm sorry to keep you waiting on your first day in school," Mrs. Oniru pacified her daughter with a peck on her cheek.

"Apology accepted. Let's be on our way. This is 2 minutes past 7:00 a.m already. I don't want to be late on my first day of school," Khadijah stated anxiously.

"Alright dear. Let's get going now," Mrs. Oniru replied, holding on to her daughter's hand.

They both walked outside to the garage. Khadijah hopped into the car and sat on the passenger's seat. Her mother grabbed the steering wheel and started the car. She zoomed off and they went to Kings and Queens College.

***

Habeebah Adetola lived with her grandmother, younger sibling and cousins. Her parents were divorced and her grandmother took their custody thereafter. Habeebah had also been admitted into the prestigious and highly regarded Kings and Queens College. Her amazing brain earned her an admission into the school for the gifted. Habeebah was a brilliant twelve-year-old girl; tall and dark in complexion with dimples that beautified her on both cheeks.

Habeebah's grandmother sold pap to make ends meet and she raised her grandkids with the meager proceeds from her pap business. Grandmother had seven of her grandchildren living with her and their parents only sent money to her once in a while. As the oldest grandchild, Habeebah always assisted her grandmother with hawking pap every morning before going to school.

The proceeds from the pap would be used to get breakfast ready every morning. If Habeebah didn't hawk in a day, breakfast would be impossible because they lived from hand to mouth.

Her grandmother promised her that once she entered secondary school, she would stop hawking pap before going to school. This was to make her concentrate on her studies.

On the morning of the school resumption day, Habeebah was excited to go to school. She woke up early to prepare breakfast. She was twelve years old and was quite dutiful with a high sense of responsibility. Living with her grandmother since she was six had made her a dutiful girl because the woman raised her to be responsible. Habeebah imbibed all she'd been taught by her grandmother, from manners to hard work, resilience and house chores duties. She'd been a great succour to her grandmother as the oldest grandchild.

The night before the resumption date, Grandmother had informed her that they would be having beans and garri to school the next day. She'd already picked the beans the previous night and woke up by 4:30 a.m the next day. Her grandmother was the landlord of the six-room house they lived in. The entrances of each room were facing each other and fitted the description of the face-to-face house.

Grandmother and her grandchildren occupied the first two rooms on the right side of the house, while tenants occupied the remaining four rooms. The toilet, bathroom and kitchen were located at the extreme of the house. The ones at the right side of the house were used by Grandmother and her grandchildren, while the remaining ones were shared by the tenants.

Habeebah walked to the end of the house where the kitchen was located to begin her cooking. She rinsed the beans, put it on the stove, and went to wake her sibling and cousins.

Habeebah had her bath and got dressed for school. She had got her school uniform during the holiday and purchased only the English textbook since her grandmother couldn't afford other subject textbooks. Her grandmother bought her necessary things she could afford and Habeebah thanked her with a grateful smile.

When she was ready to leave for school that day, her grandmother gave her fifty naira and Habeebah complained calmly, while staring at her grandmother.

"₦50 cannot be enough for me, ma. I'll eat in school and also spend money on transportation to and fro."

"How much is your transportation fare?" Grandmother asked.

"₦30 to school and ₦30 from school," Habeebah replied with a frown.

Her grandmother breathed heavily before responding.

"Okay, I'll add ₦10 to the ₦50 I already gave you. You can take food to school, you don't need to buy food in the school again," Grandmother replied.

"There's no food to take to school, grandma. I have already shared all the beans among the eight of us. Nothing is left in the pot," Habeebah replied.

"There's nothing I can do. I haven't sold anything this morning, have I? We spent the proceeds from yesterday's sales on the beans we cooked this morning. The remaining balance is what I'll share among the seven of you. Please manage. By the time you get back,

I would have made some sales. I'll get food ready for you, my darling," Grandmother pacified Habeebah.

She was appeased by Grandmother's sweet words. She thought it wouldn't be sensible to throw tantrums after the poor woman had explained the situation to her. "Hunger would not kill me in school before closing time, after all," she thought. She collected the added ₦10 from her grandmother and off she went to school.

CHAPTER TWO

The roads leading to Kings and Queens College were busy on the first day of resumption. Parents who came to drop their children in rides, parked in the school garage while their children got down from the vehicle. Students who boarded commercial vehicles to school and others who trekked all entered the school as well. They all found their ways around the school.

Kings and Queens College was a federal government school, but a sophisticated one. A well organised one with students' comfort as number one priority.

The school already provided exquisite furniture in each classroom. The old students already knew the classrooms they were promoted to. Students who arrived before assembly settled down in their classrooms without hassle.

The newly admitted JSS1 students had also known the classrooms they would belong to since they received their entrance examination results. They went into their classrooms without any inconvenience or struggle.

The first day of resumption was devoid of dragging of chairs from one classroom to another or rowdy roaming around of students. The new students were also not stranded. There were identification plates at the entrance of each classroom where the name of the classroom was boldly written.

Also, the first day of resumption was not bombarded with buying of textbooks and notebooks. These had been done during the holiday.

Khadijah got down from her mum's car at about 7:25 a.m. Her house to the school was just about a 20-minute drive. Mrs. Oniru tucked a ₦500 note in her daughter's palm. She planted a kiss on her forehead.

"Have a nice day in school," Mrs. Oniru said to her daughter with a smile.

"And you too, ma," Khadijah replied with a smile.

She bade her mum goodbye and ran along to locate her class.

Assembly would start by 7:40 a.m. Khadijah located her classroom. She sighted the plate name where JSS1A was boldly written and walked into the classroom. She met a boy in the classroom reading a book. She greeted him. The furniture in the classroom were conjoined desks and chairs which were arranged in rows. Khadijah walked up to a seat. She sat down and brought out a book too. The boy she met in the classroom probably inspired her. It was still some minutes before assembly.

Khadijah was already engrossed in her book when a short and dark complexioned boy walked in with a bang.

He greeted the class cheerfully as he walked in.

"Hello fellow students. My name is Abbas Abanikanda," the short boy greeted them with smiles, as he approached the first boy whom Khadijah met in the classroom.

"What's your name?" Abbas asked the former boy.

"My name is Hamzah Bello," the former boy, a tall, slender and dark skinned boy, replied softly.

"Nice to meet you," Abbas said to Hamzah, while walking up to Khadijah.

"My name is Abbas Abanikanda. What's your name?" Abbas asked Khadijah, who looked up from her book.

Khadijah mumbled her name. Abbas didn't hear her well. He had to ask again.

"What did you say your name is?" Abbas asked again but Khadijah ignored him and focused on her book.

Abbas shrugged and was walking away from Khadijah when two girls walked in simultaneously.

Abbas quickly went to welcome them.

"You're welcome to JSS1A. My name is Abbas Abanikanda. What are your names?" Abbas asked the girls.

"My name is Habeebah Adetola," Habeebah replied with a smile and walked past Abbas to occupy a seat.

"My name is Anat Omotosho, I am the daughter of the vice principal of this school," the second girl, a short and fair skinned girl, gallantly replied.

"Wow! That's very nice. That means you're the Very Important Personality; VIP, in our class," Abbas joked. Anat blushed with a grin.

Some other students arrived before assembly. The bell to converge the students for assembly rang at about 7:40 a.m. The students left their classrooms and headed straight to the assembly area.

The assembly area was filled with students in their beautifully garbed green and white uniforms. The female junior students were adorned with white shirts and green striped pinafores with a green beret. The male junior students wore white shirts and green striped shorts with berets. The female senior students were cladded in white shirts and green striped skirts with berets, while their male counterparts wore white shirts and green striped trousers with berets. The assembly was alluring with white and green beauties.

The assembly was conducted by the assembly prefect. The normal assembly routine was done, after which the principal walked up to the podium to address the students.

The principal welcomed the students back to school after a long vacation. She specifically welcomed the newly admitted JSS1 students. She reminded the old students about the prestige with which the school was known. She advised them to buckle down for a productive term.

The school principal, Mrs. Davies, a tall woman in her late fifties, addressed the students. Mrs. Davies informed the new students that Kings and Queens College does not condone laziness. Students of Kings and Queens College were known for their indefatigable efforts towards achieving academic excellence which had yielded fantastic and unbeatable academic records over the years.

The principal announced that there were various extra-curricular activities in the school which included clubs like: Reading Club, Future Scientists Club, Press Club, Red Cross, Islamic Religious Study group for the Muslim students, Christianity Religious Study group for the Christian students and a host of others.

The principal informed the students that they were allowed to join any club of their desire. However, she told them that the two religious study groups were compulsory for every Muslim and Christian student to join. The principal told them that knowledge about God should be given preference above all things.

Mrs. Davies also informed them that the IRK and CRK teachers would be the students' tutors in each religious study group. The other clubs' meetings would be held every Wednesday after the lunch break, while the religious study group would be held on Thursday immediately after closing hours before the after-school lesson. The principal urged the Christian students as well as the Muslim students to register with their religious knowledge teachers.

The principal dismissed the students after advising them to work hard in order to achieve the best.

***

The students of JSS1A entered their classrooms after the assembly. They all occupied available seats without any fight.

A woman in her late thirties walked into the class and announced that she was Mrs. Akorede, their class teacher. She already had their names on the class register. She addressed them about the rules of the class. She advised them to behave like good children and never flout the rules of the school and that of the classroom.

"This is secondary school. It is different from the primary school you were coming from. In primary school, your teachers are always with you in the classroom. But here, no teacher will stay with you in the classroom. Therefore, you have to behave like the good children that you are. Do not make noise when there's no teacher in your class. In the absence of a teacher, instead of staying idle or playing, take out your books and read. Do you understand?" The class teacher, Mrs. Akorede asked.

"Yes, ma'am," the students chorused.

"Alright. Please listen attentively as I call your names to mark the attendance register. If you're present, reply with 'present'. Then I'll know whoever does not respond is absent," The class teacher said and started calling out the students' names from the register.

The teacher walked out after calling the class attendance. Two students were absent from class. Aminah Badmus and Suwebah Olalekan. The class teacher asked if the other students knew why they were absent but none of them knew.

After the class teacher had left the classroom, a subject teacher walked in. The students greeted him. He introduced himself as Mr. Ige, the Mathematics teacher. He wrote the topic he would teach them on the board and went on with explanations. After he was through with the explanation, he wrote some tasks on the board and asked anyone who could solve them to raise their hands. Three students raised their hands out of the 18 students in the classroom. He was surprised.

"Does that mean it is only these three that understood the lesson?" The Mathematics teacher marvelled.

The students were quiet. Mr. Ige had to explain again. After the second explanation, he asked anyone who could solve it to raise their hands, this time, five students did. The teacher was disappointed. He wasn't pleased. If five students could only solve the task out of eighteen students, it only meant he hadn't delivered the topic perfectly.

He called upon one of the students that raised their hands. The student he called happened to be Khadijah Oniru. He asked her to come out and solve the three questions he wrote on the board. Khadijah walked out with her shoulders high. She collected the marker from the teacher and started. The teacher told her to explain as she solved the questions.

Khadijah did as instructed. She solved the questions, while explaining the steps thoroughly. The other students nodded their heads as Khadijah solved and explained the tasks. She solved all the three tasks correctly to the amazement of the teacher.

After Khadijah had finished, the other students, who didn't understand the topic earlier, exclaimed in one voice.

"Now we understand the topic perfectly, sir," the students chorused happily.

The teacher stared at Khadijah in amazement.

"Wow! That's impressive! What's your name?" The teacher asked proudly.

"My name is Khadijah Oniru, sir………," Khadijah was talking when Abbas interrupted her.

"Oniru? Do you sell locust beans in your family………?" Abbas asked with sarcasm but the teacher quickly shut him down.

"Will you keep quiet, silly boy!" The teacher instructed Abbas and then turned to Khadijah.

"Thank you, my dear. You have made me proud. Keep it up, alright!" The teacher urged Khadijah with admiration.

He instructed the class to cheer her, which they did.

The Mathematics teacher gave them some homework. His period had come to an end. He exited the class after telling the students to ensure their homework was done.

After the teacher had left, Khadijah couldn't stop smiling to herself. She loved it when she was the center of attraction. She loved the fact that she'd started displaying her brilliance early enough. The class couldn't stop admiring her as well. They were impressed by her extraordinary intelligence. Some of her classmates went to her during their free time to explain the Mathematics topic to them again, which she did cheerfully.

***

The lunch break had not arrived when Habeebah's tummy had started rumbling for food. By the time the time keeper rang the bell for the lunch break, the pang of hunger had dealt severely with her. She held her stomach as she watched her colleagues eat. She shuttled her gaze amongst them all as they ate. She salivated and wished one of them could offer her a remnant.

Khadijah brought out her luxurious food flask. She opened it and the aroma of her food filled the air. She started eating without noticing Habeebah was staring at her. It was the aroma of Khadijah's food that attracted Habeebah. She stopped staring at the others and fixed her gaze on Khadijah. Khadijah, on the other hand, didn't notice anyone was staring at her. She finished her food and closed her food flask.

Habeebah withdrew her gaze from Khadijah only after she'd closed her food flask. She hissed lightly and looked around. Every other person had finished eating. Those who didn't bring food went to get food at the school cafeteria. Even those who brought food still went out to buy refreshment. She neither had food, money to buy food nor money for refreshment. After she could no longer bear the pang of hunger, she went out to fetch some water at the school tap. The lunch break was finally coming to an end. She walked to the cafeteria hoping to see someone to beg from. She couldn't bring herself to beg. She saw Khadijah gulping a bottle of yoghurt. She wanted to move closer to her and beg but her pride held her back.

She returned to the class with the other students after the lunch break had ended. All the remaining lessons for that day fell on her deaf ears. A hungry person cannot assimilate anything.

The school closed by 2:00 p.m. The after-school lessons, which were compulsory for every student, would start by 2:20 p.m and end by 3:45 p.m. By the time it was 3:00 p.m, Habeebah could no longer hear what the teacher was saying. She sought the teacher's permission to go to the toilet. She wasn't actually going to the toilet. She had decided to spend the ₦30 which would take her home, then trek home instead.

She walked out of the classroom and headed to the cafeteria. She bought a ₦30 puff-puff. She sat on a bench in the cafeteria and devoured the puff-puff like a hungry lion. After she was through, she walked to the school tap and drank some water. She heaved a deep sigh of relief after satisfying her hungry stomach.

Habeebah walked back to the class. The teacher queried her for being late. She apologised and went back to her seat. The calmness she felt after eating was indescribable. She was able to hear what the teacher was saying loud and clear.

The lesson came to an end eventually. The students all dispersed and went their different ways.

Khadijah's mum was already waiting to pick her up at the school garage. She hopped into her mother's car excitedly. Her mum noticed her excitement and smiled.

"I can see that school was fine today, with the way my daughter is sparkling with elation," Mrs. Oniru teased her daughter.

"You can say that again, mum. I have continued my glory here as well. I did all my class work correctly. I even helped my classmates with their difficult tasks. I'm so excited, mum," Khadijah beamed with happiness.

"I'm so proud of you, my sweetheart. My daughter is the first among her peers and that makes me a proud mum. Keep it up, my dear; the sky is your starting point," Mrs. Oniru praised her daughter who continued to blush.

"Thank you, mummy," Khadijah replied with a grin. She was really feeling on top of the world.

"Shall we?" Mrs. Oniru asked her daughter.

"Yes, mum. I can't wait to get home. My stomach is grumbling for food," Khadijah said.

"Oh yes, I know. I have instructed the maid to prepare Amala and egusi soup."

"I can't wait to devour it," Khadijah said with huge anticipation.

Her mother smiled and put the gear in drive. She pressed the turtle and zoomed off.

CHAPTER THREE

Habeebah trekked the distance of 2 kilometres from the school to her house. She had no choice but to trek. She'd spent her transport fare on puff-puff. The puff-puff gave her some strength to walk home.

By the time she got back home, she was exhausted. She threw herself on the chair in her grandmother's living room and slept off. She was too tired to ask for food.

Habeebah's grandmother was not at home when she returned from school. She went to collect money from her debtors down the street. She'd promised to get food ready but she couldn't. The little sales she made since morning was spent on purchasing the raw materials for her pap production. The other grandchildren soaked some garri when they returned from school. Grandmother also left words for Habeebah to also soak garri when she returned. She was surprised when she met Habeebah sleeping.

Grandmother asked the other children if Habeebah had soaked garri but they replied that she slept immediately after she returned from school.

Habeebah woke up by 6:30 in the evening. She was really famished. She walked sluggishly to the kitchen to check if Grandmother had cooked something. To her dismay, no food was cooked. She hissed and walked out of the kitchen. She held her tummy as she felt a sting inside of her.

The aroma emanating from their tenant's kitchen stimulated her sense of smell. She walked stealthily towards their tenant's kitchen and peeped in. She saw one of their neighbour's sons, Ade, in the kitchen, doing some cooking. She sniffed the aroma hungrily. She sniffed so loudly that Ade could hear her.

Ade turned back and saw her salivating. Habeebah, upon realising Ade had caught her peeping, turned back and walked away in a tip toe.

"Come back here!" Ade's voice jolted her.

She stopped but couldn't turn back out of shame.

"Do you want some rice?" Ade offered but Habeebah shook her head.

"No, thanks," Habeebah tried to conceal her desire for Ade's food.

"Don't be silly! Your mouth says no but your eyes are telling me 'yes.' I'm studying Psychology in school, so I can tell people's emotions from their countenance. I know you're very hungry. Please don't reject the food. Don't worry, I won't tell your grandma that I gave you food," Ade convinced her, while dishing some rice for her.

He gave the plate of rice to her. Habeebah quickly grabbed it and thanked him profusely. She sneaked to the back of the house where Grandma and her siblings could not see her. She ate the food hurriedly, while looking around in case someone was coming.

When she finished eating, she washed the plate and returned it to Ade. She thanked him again for his kind gestures. Ade smiled and told her to always come to him if she needed anything. She nodded her head and smiled sheepishly.

Habeebah was relieved of her hunger after eating the plate of rice. She cleaned her mouth and walked back to Grandmother's parlour. She had the strength to do her homework. She did her homework meticulously and returned her books to her bag.

During dinner time, Grandmother was still complaining of lack of money. She told her grandchildren that she only had ₦100. She bought a ₦100 loaf of bread with the money and shared it among her seven grandchildren. She told them to eat it with water.

Habeebah collected her tiny share. She was full already but she couldn't reject it. Grandmother would get suspicious that she'd eaten something if she rejected the bread. Grandmother had nothing to eat after she had shared the loaf of bread among her grandchildren. Habeebah stared at her grandmother with sympathy. She was not hungry at all. Ade gave her plenty of rice which could sustain her till the next day. She pitied her grandmother and thought the best thing to do was to give her own tiny share of bread to her. The old woman had really been through a lot. She gave her own share of bread to Grandmother who was surprised by her action.

"Don't worry about me, Habeebah. An adult can still endure the pang of hunger but little children cannot. I'll drink some water and I'll be fine," Grandma rejected Habeebah's offer.

"Please take it, Grandma. My teacher bought plenty of food for me today because I got my classwork right. I am still full. If I eat this bread, I may have indigestion," Habeebah lied.

Grandmother was elated to hear that Habeebah got her work right. Little did she know that Habeebah lied in order for her to collect the bread. She was more excited to know that Habeebah had warmed the teacher's heart. She was pleased and proud of her. She'd always known Habeebah was a brilliant girl. She collected the bread from her and ate it with smiles. Habeebah watched her grandmother as she ate the bread and smiled too. She was happy that her grandmother would not go to bed hungry.

The early morning hawking that Habeebah stopped because of her new school was affecting the family severely. She made up her mind to continue. She would only need to work extra hard, and then she would be able to cope in school. Grandmother was too old to hawk. The other grandchildren were too little to hawk as well, which was why the responsibility of hawking was shouldered by

Habeebah alone. That evening, she told grandmother to allow her to resume hawking. That was the only way the family would not starve. Grandmother smiled and prayed for her heartily. She was really a sensible girl.

The family went to bed after dinner. In Habeebah's house, Grandmother was the only one who used to observe the five daily prayers. She didn't carry her grandchildren along. She probably thought they were still little. She forgot that the strategy to integrate little children into any activity is to catch them young. She didn't send them to *madrasah* as well. She might have thought it wasn't important.

***

Khadijah got home around 4:15 p.m. A sumptuous meal was already waiting for her. She went upstairs to her room to have a shower. She joined her parents and two siblings at the dining table after her bath.

After the meal, her dad asked how her day went. She narrated her experience on her first day in school with excitement. Her dad listened with rapt attention. He praised her for her exceptional performance. Khadijah beamed with smiles at her dad's exaltation.

Khadijah rested after her meal. At about 5:05 in the evening, her Quran teacher arrived. Her parents had got a private Quran teacher for her. They didn't allow her to attend *madrasah* outside of the house. Khadijah was their only girl and they intended to protect her like an egg.

In Khadijah's house, the five daily prayers were enjoined. The children were raised with the consciousness of *salat*. At the call to adhan, the male would go to the mosque, while Khadijah would pray at home. She'd learnt a lot from her Quran teacher. She could recite the Quran fluently. She'd equally memorized some portions of the Quran, and some *Hadiths* as well.

The Quran teacher taught her for an hour and 30 minutes. Khadijah spent the remaining time before *maghrib* to do her school homework. She couldn't finish the homework before *maghrib*. She completed it after maghrib prayer. Immediately after *ishai* prayer, she went to bed, as early to bed is early to rise.

***

The following day, Habeebah had no food to eat before going to school. Her grandmother had spent the only ₦100 she had on bread the previous night. The family woke up with no money the next day. Grandmother made some pap for her grandchildren to eat before going to school but Habeebah refused to drink the pap. Therefore, she went to school with an empty stomach. She also had no money for transportation. She had to trek to school. She knew she couldn't survive in school without food. However, she was ready to beg her classmates for food. After Ade offered her some rice the previous day, she was no longer ashamed to eat other people's food.

The students went for the morning assembly. After the assembly, they returned to their classrooms. The two students who were absent the previous day, were in school that day, Aminah and Suwebah.

That morning at the school garage when Khadijah's mum dropped her, Aminah's mother also came to drop her in a Lexus jeep. The two mothers greeted each other. Khadijah's mum whispered into her ear.

"You should make friends with that girl. They are in our calibre," Mrs. Oniru whispered to her daughter who smiled and walked up to Aminah.

"Hello! What's your name and what class are you?" Khadijah asked Aminah.

"My name is Aminah Badmus and I am in JSS1A," Aminah, a beautiful, tall and dark skinned girl, replied.

"That's my class!" Khadijah exclaimed excitedly. "My name is Khadijah Oniru. It's nice to meet you," she added with enthusiasm.

"I'm pleased to meet you too," Aminah replied to her with smiles.

"Come, let me take you to our class," Khadijah urged.

Aminah followed her with smiles.

The two girls walked to their classroom. On their way, Khadijah asked Aminah why she was absent the previous day. Aminah replied that she just returned from London the previous night.

"Wow! I visit London too for vacations. But this last vacation, I didn't go to London but Dubai," Khadijah informed her new friend proudly.

"Really! I spend vacations in Dubai too. I have some nice abayas which I got from Dubai," Aminah also informed her new friend with elation.

"I also have beautiful abayas which I got from Dubai," Khadijah expressed with pomposity.

The new friends talked about their luxurious background till they got to the class. When they got to the class, they met some students, including the other girl who was also absent the previous day, Suwebah.

Suwebah, a short and fat girl with an uneven skin tone, was eating from a very big food flask when Khadijah and Aminah got to the class. Abbas was making fun of her for bringing such a big flask to school. Suwebah replied to him with a mouth full of food.

"This is not the only flask I brought to school. I have three types of it with different foods. I'll eat one now, the second one during lunch break and the last, after school closes before the after-school lesson," Suwebah informed the class gallantly, to the amazement of Abbas.

"Wow! All the plenty of food for only you? No wonder you're fat…," Abbas was trying to tease Suwebah but Hamzah shut him down.

"It's not nice to body shame people, Abbas," Hamzah cautioned Abbas.

Abbas hissed.

"I'm not body shaming her, I'm telling her the fact. She's fat and if she doesn't cut down on her portion, she'll turn into an amoeba with no shape," Abbas teased Suwebah again.

"No, I can't turn into an amoeba. That's how I've been eating since I was born. My mother sells food. I can't eat outside. So, I always pack enough food to school right from primary school," Suwebah informed them again.

"I see. Just don't spoil the school's toilet with plenty of feces, because the more you eat, the more you'll excrete waste," Abbas joked.

Suwebah rolled her eyes at him. She continued eating her food, unperturbed.

Immediately after Khadijah and Aminah walked into the class, Abbas rushed to meet them and greeted them cheerfully. Khadijah snubbed him and walked to her seat. Aminah returned his greetings with smiles.

"You were absent yesterday," Abbas said to Aminah."

"Yes," Aminah replied courteously and walked to an empty seat.

By the time Habeebah could get to school, the morning assembly had almost ended. After the morning assembly, the first period came and ended without her active performance in class. The second period also came and ended without her paying attention in class. She was distracted. Her hungry stomach couldn't allow her to concentrate on the lesson. She put her head on the table while the lesson was going on.

The teacher moved over to her. He shouted at her for sleeping in the middle of a lesson. He asked her to be on her feet so that she wouldn't sleep again. Habeebah was on her feet till the end of the lesson. Her legs were shaking vigorously but the teacher didn't notice.

By the time the third period crept in, Habeebah could no longer endure the hunger. She held her stomach in pain. She managed to survive till the lunch break.

The lunch break came and the students who brought food to school brought out their meals to eat. Those who didn't bring food went out to get food or snacks. Habeebah looked round the classroom. She surveyed her colleagues one after the other, while salivating. She checked out for who to go to. Eventually, she couldn't bring herself to go to anyone. She was too ashamed to beg.

The lunch break was finally coming to an end. Habeebah writhed in pain as the pang of hunger stung her stomach. She was still writhing in pain when she heard Suwebah asking for who could assist her to write her names on all her textbooks and notebooks.

Abbas replied to Suwebah with an insulting joke.

"It is only food you know how to eat. To write your name on your books is difficult for you, FFO," Abbas remarked jokingly.

"You better keep quiet!" Suwebah responded to Abbas harshly. "Do you know how many books I've got? I have 10 textbooks and 25 notebooks to write my names on. I can't write it because my finger is just healing from a whitlow infection. I also have accumulated notes. Whoever can do everything for me will receive a ₦500 note for the work," Suwebah offered. This made Habeebah to quickly get up from her seat and rushed to Suwebah's seat.

"I'll do everything for you. Yes, I will," Habeebah emphasised.

"Are you sure?" Suwebah asked.

"Yes, I'm sure," Habeebah replied with a nod.

"Okay, let me see your handwriting first. I don't want illegible handwriting," Suwebah demanded.

Habeebah rushed to her seat to get her notebook.

She showed it to Suwebah, who nodded her head satisfactorily.

"You have beautiful handwriting. I'll give you the money after everything is done," Suwebah said.

"No, it's payment before service," Habeebah replied with a strong will.

"Hahaha! Why should I pay you before the service is rendered?" Suwebah protested.

"That's my condition," Habeebah replied obstinately. She couldn't wait to get hold of the money and then rush to fill her hungry stomach with food.

"Okay. I'll give you the money but my work must be done before tomorrow morning," Suwebah requested.

"Of course. I'll take it home and finish everything before tomorrow morning. Give me the money now please!" Habeebah demanded, spreading out her palm.

Suwebah brought out a ₦500 note and gave it to Habeebah. She rushed out immediately to get some food.

She bought the biggest plate of rice and sachet water. She ate her fill and burped. She couldn't stop being thankful to God who sent Suwebah as a helper. Though the help was not free of charge, it came with a task but she was still grateful. She was still eating when the time-keeper rang the bell for the end of the lunch break. She finished her food in haste and returned to the class.

By the time she got back to the classroom, another period had started. She walked to her seat with vigour. She participated actively in class. She did her classwork heartily and got everything right. After the lesson, she collected Suwebah's books and began the task she'd been paid for.

Habeebah would stop writing whenever a teacher entered the classroom, and continued whenever the lesson had ended. She continued writing for Suwebah for the next few weeks, while getting paid. The workload on her head doubled as she had to write her notes, then Suwebah's notes too. She always took Suwebah's notebooks home to write. She would stay up late before going to bed.

Even in school, she joggled between her own work and that of Suwebah. The task was burdensome but she couldn't stop because she needed the money Suwebah was offering her. Her grandmother would not stop complaining of lack of money. A lot of times, they only had pap to drink before going to school. A lot of times also, there was no availability of transport fare to school. If not because of Suwebah's money, she would have gone hungry and trekked to and from school so many times. Even after Suwebah's whitlow had completely healed, she didn't stop giving her notes to Habeebah to write for her. She was enjoying it and had become so lazy.

However, the exchange between Habeebah and Suwebah stopped when the Integrated science teacher discovered what was going on between them. The teacher scolded both of them for doing such a silly thing in the school. Habeebah went back to her previous hard life of living in lack, while Suwebah buckled down and started writing her notes by herself.

***

The Muslim students attended the Islamic Religious Study Group every Thursday. They learnt about the Islamic religion. Their tutors took them through the Quran, *Hadith*, *Fiqh*, *Seerah* and other aspects of Islamic knowledge.

On Thursday of the first week of resumption, the IRK teacher, Mrs Abisoye, took them through *Seerah*. They learnt about the life of a female *Sahabiyyah*, named, Umm Sulaym bint Malhan-Rumaisa(RA)

Mrs Abisoye narrated that Umm Sulaym bint Malhan-Rumaisa, may Allah be pleased with her, was the mother of a famous companion, Anas bin Malik (RA). She converted to Islam before her whole family and her husband divorced her as a result. She was able to direct her son towards Islam.

When Anas ibn Malik turned 10 years of age, Umm Sulaym took him to the Prophet (PBUH) and offered him to his service. The Prophet admitted him to his household where Anas stayed for 10 years and hence, the reason we have so many narrations of hadith from Anas.

Anas reported that Umm Sulaim said to the Prophet (PBUH) 'here is your servant, Anas, invoke the blessings of Allah upon him.' Thereupon, the Prophet said: "O Allah, make an increase in his wealth, and progeny, and confer blessings upon him in everything thou hast bestowed upon him." It's said that Anas bin Malik then lived on for 100 years as a rich man and had 100 children and grandchildren.

Umm Sulaim married another companion then, Anas said: "Abu Talhah married Umm Sulaim and the dowry between them was Islam. She became a Muslim before him, and he proposed to her but she said: 'I have become a Muslim; if you become a Muslim, I'll marry you." So he became a Muslim and that was the dowry between them." Narrated Jabir bin `Abdullah: (RA), The Prophet (PBUH) said, "I saw myself (in a dream) entering Paradise, and behold! I saw Ar-Rumaisa," Abu Talha's wife.'

The statement of the prophet indicated that Allah is pleased with Umm Sulaim and that He would admit her into paradise. Umm Sulaim's life is a model for Muslims to follow.

A lot of lessons are to be learnt in the story of Umm Sulaim, such as: If a mother wants her child to learn a skill, then as long as she's passionate about it, she should embark on it, Allah will help her to reach her goal.

It's said that Umm Sulaim was so passionate about Islam that she went to a battle with full term pregnancy.

Another important lesson in the story of Umm Sulaim is that there's nothing wrong in converting to Islam when marrying someone. And as opposed to the popular belief of women converting for men, here we see an example of a rich, skillful man, converting to Islam for a seemingly poor, divorced woman. Of course, he converted for the sake of Allah, but it was her offer that he considered which led him to Islam," Mrs Abisoye concluded.

She then threw questions at the students about what they learnt from the story?

A female student responded.

"I learnt that a Muslim should submit everything she has to the worship of Allah," Aminah Badmus said.

"That's very correct," Mrs. Abisoye responded to Aminah.

"I learnt that a Muslim should be steadfast. Umm Sulaim was steadfast and that was why she didn't agree to marry a *kaffir*," Khadijah Oniru expressed.

"You're right," Mrs Abisoye remarked.

"I learnt that mothers should educate their children in the way of God as evident in how Ummu Sulaim took her son, Anas, to the prophet, (PBUH)," Anat stated.

"You're right. Wait, why are the girls the only ones responding, are there no boys in this class?" Mrs. Abisoye marvelled.

Abbas responded to her.

"The story is a female story; that's why the boys are not responding," Abbas said to the astonishment of the teacher, who laughed out before correcting Abbas' wrong notion.

"The story is a female story, that's true. But that doesn't mean the lesson inherent in the story is not for both genders. In fact, the lessons in the story are for all Muslims to imbibe, regardless of gender. Now I want the boys to tell me what they have learnt from the story," Mrs. Abisoye urged them.

Hamzah was the first to speak.

"I learnt that children should always obey their parents. Anas obeyed his mother when she took him to the prophet, (PBUH), to serve him," Hamzah responded.

"That's very correct. Children should obey their parents at all times. Anas' obedience led him to success in this life and the next. When children obey their parents, Allah will be pleased with them. With these, we'll end the class. Hope to see you by next Thursday, In-shaa-Allah," Mrs. Abisoye said and dismissed the students.

The class was interesting and educational. The students learnt a lot.

CHAPTER FOUR

During the second week of the term, the Home Economics teacher, Mrs. Omolara, walked into the JSS1A classroom. She wrote the topic of the week on the board. The students exchanged glances when they saw PUBERTY. The word was new to some of them, while a few of them were already familiar with the word.

The students were too shy to ask questions from the teacher. After the teacher was done, she asked that whoever had questions should ask but none of the students responded. Mrs. Omolara assumed that they understood the topic. She called it a day.

The topic was an eye-opener for the students. It made them realised that there was something called puberty. Some of the students, especially the girls, were too shy to ask the teacher questions. They were conscious of the boys' presence. Khadijah Oniru, upon getting home, decided to ask her mum the questions she couldn't ask the teacher in class.

"Mummy," Khadijah started.

"Yes darling," Mrs. Oniru replied to her daughter.

"We were taught puberty in school today," Khadijah informed her mother. And this time, Mrs. Oniru left what she was doing to give her daughter maximum attention.

"Interesting topic you have there! Did you find it interesting?" Mrs. Oniru was curious.

"No," Khadijah replied without vigour, and this time, her mother paid more attention to her gestures.

"Why didn't you find it interesting? The topic used to be a very fascinating one back in the day."

"It's not fascinating at all. I can't relate with all the things that the teacher said," Khadijah replied.

"Oops! Sorry about that. What are the things that were strange to you from the discussion?" Mrs. Oniru asked.

"Everything. The body changes, especially because I haven't experienced any," Khadijah said, raising her brow.

"Oh, that's true. Don't worry. You're only nine. When you grow older, you'll experience everything that the teacher discussed in the puberty class, okay?"

"Yes, ma."

"Now, ask me anything that you don't understand about the topic," Mrs Oniru urged her daughter.

"The teacher explained puberty as the time in which a child's sexual and physical characteristics mature. It occurs due to hormone changes. Mrs. Omolara also explained that adolescence is the period between puberty and adulthood. I don't understand at all," Khadijah said wryly.

"Okay darling. Don't worry at all. Mummy is here for you. I'll explain everything in the language you'll understand. You see my dear, in simple terms, puberty is the transition from childhood to adulthood. It is when your body experience changes because you're growing up. When a baby is born, the baby grows from a tiny baby to a bigger one, day by day. The same applies to puberty. It simply means growing up from a child to becoming an adult. Puberty is a normal part of growing up, and each person's experience of it is unique. Do you understand?"

"Yes, mum, please continue," Khadijah replied anxiously.

"Okay. You see, the exact age a child enters puberty depends on a number of different things, such as genes, nutrition, and gender......."

"Mummy, what is gene? I understand that nutrition is the food we eat and gender is our sex. But what is gene?" Khadijah asked curiously.

Her mum smiled before responding.

"Okay, I'll explain what a gene means in a simple language you'll understand. A gene is a basic unit of heredity in a living organism. Genes come from our parents. We may inherit our physical traits, such as shape of eyes, nose, mouth, head, legs and other physical features from our parents. Can you see that my nose and yours are similar?"

"Yes, mummy. They are."

"Good. That's genes."

"Okay. Now I understand," Khadijah expressed wholeheartedly.

Her mum stroked her hair and continued.

"We may also have the likelihood of getting certain diseases and conditions from a parent, that's genes too," Mrs. Oniru said.

"Condition like what, mummy?" Khadijah asked curiously.

"Well, let's use menstruation as an example. I started my menstruation quite late, at age 15. There's a likelihood that you'll start late as well, that's genes at work," Mrs. Oniru explained.

"Now I get it. Please continue," Khadijah pleaded.

"Puberty in girls is different from that of boys. In girls, breast development is the main sign that a girl is entering puberty. The breast will start to grow bigger."

"I haven't experienced that, mum," Khadijah complained sharply.

"Don't worry, you will. You're just nine. If you take after my gene like I explained earlier, your puberty might be slow," Mrs. Oniru explained.

"Hmmm, okay," Khadijah replied unsatisfactorily. It seemed she wanted to grow up fast since she'd learnt about puberty.

Her mother continued.

"After breast growth comes menstruation. Menstruation is the monthly flow of blood from the uterus. Menstruation starts in some girls as early as eight years."

"Eight years?" Khadijah marvelled. "That's fast!"

"It's not fast, dear. Gene can also influence the start of menstruation," Mrs. Oniru explained.

"I see. Please continue, mummy," Khadijah urged her mother pleadingly.

"Before the first menstrual period, a girl will normally have: an increase in height, an increase in hip size, clear or whitish vaginal discharge, pubic and armpit hair growth......"

"You mean I'll have hair underneath my armpit and private part?" Khadijah interrupted sharply.

"Of course," Mrs. Oniru replied.

Khadijah squeezed her face.

"Yuck!" Khadijah expressed disgust.

Her mum burst into laughter.

"Look at this girl, *o*. It's part of growth and being a normal human being."

"Anyone who does not have hair underneath the armpit and private part is abnormal?" Khadijah marvelled.

"Well, I don't know. Scientists will have to explain that to us," Mrs. Oniru tried to dodge the question. She smiled at her daughter.

Khadijah wore an unsatisfied expression.

"Please tell me more about menstruation," Khadijah requested politely.

"Okay. After menstruation starts, the ovaries begin to produce and release eggs......"

"What are ovaries?" Khadijah interrupted sharply.

Her mum turned her face to one side and muttered to herself: "I'm really done for, today," Mrs. Oniru muttered.

"What did you say, mummy?"

"Never mind. What was your last question?" Mrs. Oniru asked, pretending not to hear her daughter's last question.

"You said, after menstruation, the ovaries begin to produce and release eggs, I don't know what ovaries mean. What are ovaries?" Khadijah repeated her question.

Her mum sighed deeply before responding.

"Well, let's just say ovaries are a part of a woman's organ which produces hormones…..,"

"What are hormones?" Khadijah interrupted sharply.

"Wow! I didn't prepare for this hot seat, Khadijah!" Her mother frowned.

"Please tell me, mummy," she pleaded.

"Well, hormones are special chemicals our body makes to help it do certain things like- grow up! Hormones can't be separated from puberty. Hormones are important when our body starts to go through puberty," Mrs Oniru explained.

"Okay," Khadijah replied.

"Alright. As I was saying, ovaries are a part of a woman's organ which produces hormones for breast development, body shape, body hair, menstrual cycle, fertility, and pregnancy."

"And pregnancy?" Khadijah asked, surprised.

"Yes, and pregnancy. That's because a girl who has started menstruation can become pregnant with a man's touch. For this reason, do not allow a man to touch you," Mrs. Oniru said. Khadijah marvelled.

"Do you mean touch, as in, ordinary body contact?" Khadijah asked.

"No, not ordinary body contact. But ordinary and carefree body contact can lead to more dangerous contact. That is why ordinary body contact should be avoided in totality. Do you understand?"

"Yes, ma. Perfectly."

"That's good. Anything else?"

"I also want to know about boy's puberty."

"Are you a boy?" Mrs. Oniru teased her.

"No. But I just want to know."

"Alright. I'll tell you. Boys will experience faster growth, especially height. Hair growth under the armpit, on the face; like moustache and beard. Boys will also grow hair in the pubic area. Boys will have an increased shoulder width and deep voice. They'll experience the growth of the penis and scrotum and more. Puberty is not only physical growth and change, but also emotional, psychological, social, and mental change and growth," Mrs. Oniru said.

The last sentence was not clear to Khadijah, so she asked questions.

"Puberty is not only physical growth and change, but also emotional, psychological, social, and mental change and growth, please explain, mummy!"

"Okay. You know physical growth is the development of breast, pubic hair, armpit hair, menstruation, moustache, deep voice, increased shoulder width and so on, these are growths that you can see with your eyes, this is why we call them physical growth. Puberty also brings some changes that you can only feel and perceive. These changes are the mental, psychological, social and emotional growth. Emotional growth is when you become more sensible. You no longer disturb mummy and daddy to buy you things that are not necessary. You become more understanding of life's situations. You become calmer and wiser. That's emotional growth."

Khadijah grinned.

"I perfectly understand. You're the best, mummy. What's social growth?"

"Social growth is when you become more aware of happenings around you and you want to partake in them. For instance, school leadership like head-girl, head-boy and other positions assist children to be socially responsible. Social growth is also the improvement in your understanding of others, and your attitudes and behaviours towards them as well."

Khadijah nodded her head satisfactorily.

"Psychological and mental growth are yet to be explained, mummy!"

"Yes, darling. Mental growth is the development of your intelligence. The way you perceive things, your observation of things, your imaginations, your thoughts, your ability to provide solutions to problems become matured. Mental growth generally refers to the overall growth of your intellectual capacity. And psychological growth is the combination of the other aforementioned three, social, emotional and mental growth. Do you understand the topic now, my darling?" Mrs. Oniru asked her daughter.

"Yes, very well, mummy, better than the teacher's explanation."

"I'm glad you do. You didn't understand the teacher not because the teacher's explanation was flawed but because you didn't ask questions."

"I was shy?"

"I know. And that is why I'm here for you always. A child is always freer with the mother. Don't hesitate to ask me anything, okay!"

"Yes, mummy. Thank you so much, mummy. You're the best," Khadijah appreciated her mum with a hug.

CHAPTER FIVE

r. Ige, the Mathematics teacher, walked into JSS1A on a Tuesday afternoon. He looked round the classroom with smiles. The students wondered why he was smiling. At last, he spoke to them.

"I'm very happy to announce to you that the school has been invited to a Mathematics competition which will come up 2 weeks from now. I am also elated to tell you that we already have representatives for the Junior Category," Mr. Ige informed the students with smiles.

The students were curious to know who the representatives were. Therefore, they asked in unison.

"Who are the representatives, sir?" The class chorused.

"Good question! The three students who will be representing the school in the junior category of the Mathematics competition are Khadijah, Habeebah and Hamzah," Mr. Ige announced.

The class went into a spree of murmuring.

"Silence!" Mr. Ige instructed, and the class maintained silence.

Mr. Ige continued speaking.

"I came up with the decision to pick the trio of Khadijah, Habeebah and Hamzah after carefully observing their Mathematics performance, both in the classroom and homework since the beginning of this term. I can say it, without mincing words, that those three are gifted. Therefore, there would be no better representatives for this competition than them. I'm certain that they will make the school proud by winning the competition," Mr. Ige concluded.

Before Mr. Ige left the classroom, he informed the three chosen students about the preparation for the competition which would take place every morning henceforth, for 45 minutes before the morning assembly. That simply meant that the students were expected to be in school every day by 7:00 a.m.

Khadijah was happy that she'd been chosen among the best three. She couldn't wait to inform her parents about it. She would definitely make the 7:00 a.m scheduled time for the preparation of the competition.

Habeebah was happy too to have been chosen among the best three. Despite the workload on her head, she was still able to perform excellently in school. However, she was worried that the early morning hawking of pap which the family had survived on, would be affected.

Habeebah always woke up by 4:30 a.m every day, after which she would do some house chores. Then take her bath and set out to hawk pap by 5:30 a.m. Pap is an early morning business. The target customers would still be at home at that time which was why the early morning sales were always good. She became worried that the family would go back to suffering for the two weeks she would be coming early to school.

She decided to tell the Mathematics teacher that she wasn't interested in the competition. Her family's comfort was her first priority before anything.

After school closed that day before the after-school lesson, she went to see the Mathematics teacher in the staff room. She told him that she would not be able to partake in the competition. She didn't explain her reasons. The teacher dismissed her after informing her that her name had already been registered for the competition. There was no way she could opt out.

Habeebah walked out of the office unsatisfactorily. She decided not to stop the pap hawking but reschedule her time to accommodate the new routine. She would wake up henceforth by 4:00 a.m. She would do whatever that needed to be done and then set out to hawk by 5:15 a.m instead of 5:30 a.m. She would try to get back before 6:00 a.m, take breakfast and head to school.

That new time-table was the only way her family would not go hungry and which would also afford her the opportunity to partake in the competition.

***

Khadijah informed her mother when she came to pick her up after school about the competition. Her mother was happy to know that her daughter was excelling in school. She encouraged her to work hard for the competition in order to bring glory to the school. Her mother also pledged her support. She promised to always get up early so as to meet up with her daughter's new routine.

Khadijah thanked her mother with smiles. The woman had always been her biggest fan.

Mother and daughter got home after a few minutes of driving. As usual, a nice meal had been waiting for them. They both went to their separate rooms to take a shower.

The family ate together on the dining table. Khadijah returned to her room to observe a siesta. Her siesta came to an end with the arrival of her Quran teacher. She joined the Quran teacher downstairs and a session of spiritual education began.

That day, the Quran teacher educated Khadijah about empathy.

The teacher began by explaining the meaning of empathy to her.

"Empathy is the ability to put yourself in someone else's shoes and understand their emotions. It is thinking about others, understanding their mindset, identifying and feeling their distress. Empathy is a step towards compassion. Empathy is a powerful tool that can bring about tranquility and goodwill to this world that is filled with so much hatred and animosity," the teacher explained.

Khadijah nodded her head.

"Please give me a practical example of empathy," Khadijah requested of the teacher.

"Hmmmmmmm.......the practical example of empathy can be seen in the life of our noble prophet Muhammad (PBUH). For example, the Prophet (PBUH) would shorten his congregational prayer when he hears the wails of a child. Just because a lengthy one would distress the mother. The prophet put himself in the mother's shoes and tried to understand her pains. And the best he could do is to shorten the prayer so that mother and child could be fine. This is one out of numerous examples of empathy that can be found in the life of our noble prophet (PBUH)," the teacher explicated.

"How can we show empathy to people?" Khadijah asked.

"For your own level, you can show empathy by encouraging your classmate who failed a test or exam that better days are ahead of her. Do not mock anyone that fails, rather, put yourself in their shoes and imagine their pains. Say soothing words to them and assist them to study if you're better than them in a particular subject or topic. You can also show empathy by trying your best to take people out of difficulties. If you have an extra pen, share with your friend that has none. If you have extra money, share it with your friend that has none," the teacher explained.

Khadijah nodded her head.

"How do I know who doesn't have money or an extra pen if they do not ask for assistance?" Khadijah asked.

The teacher smiled before answering her.

"Well, you can know by observation. When you observe happenings around you then you know those who need help. If you can, extend your hand of solidarity to them and Allah will reward you abundantly," the teacher explained further.

***

Habeebah informed her grandmother that she'd been chosen among the three students that would represent the school in a competition. She informed Grandmother that she had to get to school by 7:00 a.m for the next two weeks, in preparation for the competition. Grandmother was happy and proud of Habeebah. Grandmother suggested that Habeebah should stop the early morning hawking to enable her to get to school early but Habeebah objected. She told Grandmother that she would cope fine. Grandmother smiled and prayed for her profusely. Habeebah had proved herself to be a jewel of inestimable value.

The next morning, Habeebah woke up by 4:00 a.m as she had planned. She did some house chores and when it was quarter past 5:00 a.m, she carried the tray of pap on her head and went out to hawk.

She returned by 5:50 a.m. She used the money she realised from the sales to buy some cups of rice. She put the rice on the stove and went to take her bath. The food was done before 6:30 a.m. She dished her own portion in her food flask and hurried to school. She was able to get to school by two minutes before 7:00.a.m.

Khadijah and Hamzah were already waiting in the classroom. Habeebah quickly took a seat, as she panted heavily due to the rush she went through.

Khadijah observed the way she was panting and thought she must have gone through some stress while coming to school. She moved closer to her and asked why she was late but Khadijah's question got on Habeebah's nerves.

"Am I late like this? This is two minutes before 7:00 a.m. Even the teacher is not here yet. And you're here asking me a silly question!" Habeebah snapped at Khadijah, who felt embarrassed and returned to her seat.

Khadijah was only trying to put what her Quran teacher taught her the previous day into practice. She saw a classmate who was panting heavily and decided to show concern. She didn't know her action would get on her nerves.

Mr. Ige, the Mathematics teacher, walked into the classroom at exactly 7:00 a.m. He took them through the lesson for the next 45 minutes before the bell for the morning assembly interrupted the class. He called it a day with them. The three of them went to join their mates at the assembly.

The early morning preparation-lesson continued. The three chosen students always arrived on time also. Habeebah tried her best. She didn't find it so easy but she was determined not to stop the hawking because of the early morning class. She joggled both well for a week before an unexpected occurrence happened during the following week.

CHAPTER SIX

During the second week of the preparation-lesson, Habeebah woke up early as usual. She did her normal routine and set out for hawking at exactly 5:15 a.m. She walked through the streets and paused at every house to advertise her sale.

"Ekaaro ologi de o," she would announce at every house.

She walked through the dark street. There was no electricity. She always held a small torch to light her way. She'd been hawking pap within that locality since she was seven. So, somehow, she wasn't afraid of the darkness because she was well conversant with the locality.

She advertised her sale as she walked from street to street. The people who needed pap would come out and buy from her. Those who do not need pap would dismiss her with a prayer that she would have a fruitful sale.

She trekked more streets in order to make more sales. She made quite a good sale that morning. She was really excited. She was heading home when a bike man barricaded her. She paused and asked if he needed some pap. The bike man nodded his head. Habeebah asked the amount he wanted. He replied that he wanted ₦50 worth of pap. Habeebah was excited. She picked a ₦50 worth of pap and handed it to the bike man.

The bike man grabbed her hand and covered her nose with a handkerchief that had been laced with sedative. She fell unconscious immediately and dropped the tray of pap on the floor. The bike man carried her unto the front of the bike so that he could hold her firmly since she was unconscious. He climbed the bike and zoomed off.

Habeebah opened her eyes in an uncompleted building. She didn't know where she was or how she got there. She tried to move but she realised that she'd been tied. Her hands and legs had been tied with a rope. She couldn't scream either because her mouth had been sealed with tape.

She looked round the uncompleted building but couldn't see anyone. She groaned and moaned in pain. She hummed since she couldn't speak but that didn't help. She continued to struggle in tears. She was confused. The last thing she remembered was when she wanted to give the bike man the pap he requested. She couldn't tell how she got into an uncompleted building. She knew she was in danger. She cried bitterly.

Back at home, Grandmother expected Habeebah to have been back before 6:00 a.m but didn't see her. The time ticked till it was past six, yet Habeebah was out of sight. She waited impatiently. She paced up and down the house till it was 6:30 a.m, yet Habeebah didn't return. Grandmother was beginning to get worried. She went outside the house to check on her but Habeebah was nowhere to be seen. Grandmother waited outside for over 30 minutes, yet Habeebah didn't return. When it was past seven, she ran inside the house to inform her tenants that Habeebah had not returned.

Grandmother's tenants showed sympathy. They were surprised that Habeebah wasn't back at that time. They decided to go look for her. They divided themselves in twos and went in search of Habeebah.

They searched the nooks and crannies of the community while shouting Habeebah's name. The people who saw Habeebah that morning, testified that she passed through their houses. The people who bought pap from her that morning also testified that they saw her. The community joined in the search for Habeebah. They looked everywhere for her to no avail. They only saw her tray. Then they knew something had happened to her.

The tenants returned home after a frantic and fruitless search for Habeebah. They informed Grandmother that they couldn't find Habeebah. Grandmother cried bitterly. She hit herself as she cried amidst hot lamentations. The neighbours advised Grandmother to lodge a complaint at the police station. Grandmother and some of the neighbours went to the police station but they were told a person could not be declared missing until 24 hours had passed.

Upon hearing that, Grandmother broke into tears again. The neighbours consoled her. They returned home and resumed a fresh search for Habeebah. Grandmother put a call through to Habeebah's parents to inform them of the unfortunate incident. Her parents screamed at the other end of the phone. They promised to visit Grandmother as soon as possible to do the search for Habeebah together.

It was already 2:00 p.m, Habeebah's parents had arrived. Her mother cried bitterly. Her father lamented. They searched all the corners of the community for Habeebah without success. Grandmother had already cried her eyes out. She was inconsolable, especially when Habeebah's father blamed her for what happened.

One of Grandmother's tenants, Mama Akin, who knew how Grandmother had been toiling hard to survive with her grandchildren, scolded Habeebah's father never to blame Grandmother for what happened.

"This is never Grandmother's fault. The old woman always tries her best to raise her grandchildren. This wouldn't have happened if you as Habeebah's father had stood up to your responsibilities by sending money regularly to this old woman. This wouldn't have happened if the remaining fathers of her grandchildren had stood up to their responsibilities as well. But no, you people just left your responsibilities to Grandmother without looking back. You know this woman doesn't have any other source of living except this pap business, yet you abandoned her with many grandchildren with little or no support. Don't blame Grandmother at all. Blame yourself for being a deadbeat father," Mama Akin expressed harshly to Habeebah's father.

Habeebah's father replied to Mama Akin rudely.

"Please, don't interfere in our family matters! If I had money, I would have been sending it to Grandmother to take care of my children. But I don't have money and I can't kill myself...," Habeebah's father was speaking but her mother interrupted him with tears in her eyes.

"Do you ever have money in your life? Having no money has always been your excuse for being irresponsible. You are simply irresponsible, stop blaming your irresponsibility on lack of money. I left you because of this carefree attitude. You always spend your money on women and alcohol, tell me how you'll ever have money.....?" Habeebah's mother shouted.

Habeebah's dad interrupted fiercely.

"Don't ever disrespect me. If you disrespect me, I'll slap you," Habeebah's dad uttered angrily.

His ex-wife hissed loudly at him.

"If you dare slap me, you'll rot in jail, you this good-for-nothing man," Habeebah's mum replied.

Seeing that it was becoming a hot argument, Grandmother shouted at both of them.

"The two of you should keep quiet! Do you have any sense at all? Your daughter is missing and here you are, fighting like little children. Save your fight till my granddaughter is found. Otherwise, both of you can get out of my house!" Grandmother shouted with tears in her eyes.

Habeebah's parents kept quiet. The family deliberated on the next line of action.

***

Habeebah was still struggling to loosen herself from the captivity of the ropes she was tied with. She couldn't untie herself. Neither could she remove the tape on her mouth. The tape on her mouth was preventing her from shouting for help. She had cried so much that her tears had stopped flowing. She wondered what state her family would be in by now. Her poor Grandmother would have cried so much. Her parents would have been contacted. They would have worried a lot. Grandmother's tenants would also have stressed so much to look for her. In short, the whole community would have been thrown into disarray.

She looked around her again, there was no one in the uncompleted building. Since she woke up several hours ago, no one had come into the building as well. Habeebah could hear footsteps from passersby but there was no way she could shout for help. She continued to cry. She prayed solemnly for a miracle to happen. She doesn't want to die.

She was really very hungry. She'd had nothing to eat since daybreak and it appeared it was evening already, judging by the long hours she'd spent there. In this situation, she needed nothing but safety. She could endure hunger but she wouldn't be able to imagine being separated from her family or eventually being killed. She cried bitterly for her life. She remembered the Mathematics competition and cried even more. She prayed to God to save her from the calamity which was about to befall her.

Habeebah had heard so many stories about kidnapping. She never imagined it could happen to her. She'd heard numerous unpleasant stories about how kidnappers killed their victims and removed their organs for rituals. She cried more at the thought of her organs

58

being removed for rituals. She was still lost in thought when she started hearing footsteps drawing closer to her. She maintained silence and observed where the footsteps were coming from. The footsteps were getting nearer until two men appeared before her.

She quickly recognised one as the bike man that kidnapped her. She murmured but the bike man instructed her to keep quiet. The bike man turned to the other man and spoke to him.

"This is the meat I got for you. An organ each is ₦100,000. I'll prepare the meat tomorrow morning and remove the organs before you arrive," the bike man said to the second man. Habeebah was frightened by what she just heard, she screamed underneath her sealed mouth.

She shuddered at the thought of being killed. She cried bitterly at the thought of being butchered like an animal. She screamed loudly underneath the sealed mouth. The bike man snapped at her.

"I asked you to keep quiet! Even if you shout from now till tomorrow, no one is going to hear you. So, it's better you keep quiet for your own good," the bike man shouted at Habeebah, who continued to scream without listening to him.

The other man intervened.

"Has she eaten anything since daybreak?" The other man asked.

"No, she hasn't. She's going to die tomorrow anyway, what's the need for her to eat?" The bike man replied heartlessly.

"No. That's not good enough. Please give her something to eat," the other man urged the bike man.

"If we unseal her mouth, she's going to scream. And passersby will hear her; that's my fear," the bike man said, while the second man turned to Habeebah.

"Excuse me little girl, do you want to eat or not? You have two options here. It's either we unseal your mouth so that you can eat, on the condition that you'll not shout, or you remain hungry till you meet your end if you want to shout," the second man said sternly.

Habeebah ignored them, she continued screaming and crying.

"Please leave her, she's not hungry at all. She cannot die before tomorrow. And even if she dies, that will only make our work easier," the bike man said meanly, as Habeebah's tears dropped effortlessly.

"Alright then. I'll be on my way," the other man said and took his leave.

The bike man stared at Habeebah with scorn. He sat down and made some phone calls. He told his recipients that organs would be available the next day. Habeebah shivered with fear when he heard that again. Bitter salty tears cascaded her cheeks. She pitied herself for being a victim of circumstance. She pitied her grandmother who would be more bereaved by her death. She continued crying, while the bike man shouted at her to keep quiet.

After some minutes, the bike man got up to leave.

"I'm leaving. I'll see you tomorrow. There's no way you can escape, so don't even try to be smart," the bike man said viciously and left.

Habeebah cried non-stop. By this time, she couldn't even feel the pang of hunger. She wept bitterly. She was close to her mortality. She struggled to free herself from the rope but she couldn't. She cried non-stop into the night.

***

Back in Grandmother's house, it was already evening. Habeebah's family and neighbours had searched everywhere for her without success. Her grandmother had cried gallons of tears. Her mother had cried till her eyes were swollen. Even her dad who was initially acting like a man eventually broke down in tears; a whole child was missing. The neighbours consoled the family but they were inconsolable.

The Imam of their community mosque was also in their house to pay them a solidarity visit. He prayed for the safe return of Habeebah. He also urged the family to pray to Allah, and put their faith in Him. The Imam admonished them to have absolute reliance on Allah in their situation. The Imam assured them that Allah who saved Prophet Yunus (AS) from the belly of the whale would surely save Habeebah from whatever danger she might be in. The words of the Imam didn't resonate with the family. They were just weeping like bereaved. However, the Imam continued to admonish them to be patient and pray for their daughter's safe return.

The family waited impatiently to receive a call from the kidnappers. They thought if Habeebah was kidnapped for ransom, the kidnappers would have called to demand for a ransom. When they didn't receive any call till late evening, they were all terrified. They feared their daughter might have been kidnapped for rituals. This thought scared them terribly. They cried and wailed helplessly.

When it was exactly 7:05 in the evening, Grandmother's brother arrived. He told the family that he knew a fortune teller who could tell them exactly where Habeebah was. The family was ready to go to any length in order to find Habeebah. They won't mind visiting a fortune teller, if that would bring back their daughter. Grandmother and Habeebah's parents were ready to follow Grandmother's brother. The three of them all got up to follow him immediately but the Imam stopped them.

The Imam told them to rely solely on Allah and not seek help from His creatures. The Imam sprung into a spiritual admonition. He quoted the *Hadith* of the Prophet (PBUH) about the forbiddance of seeking help from soothsayers or fortune tellers.

"Aishah (May Allah be pleased with her) said: Some people asked the Messenger of Allah (PBUH) about soothsayers. He (PBUH) said, "They are of no account." Upon this, they said to him, "O Messenger of Allah! But they sometimes make true predictions." Thereupon the Messenger of Allah (PBUH) said, "That is a word pertaining to truth which a jinn snatches (from the angels) and whispers into the ears of his friend (the soothsayers) who will then mix more than a hundred lies with it," [Al-Bukhari and Muslim], the Imam quoted and continued.

"Safiyyah, daughter of Abu `Ubaid, narrated, on the authority of some of the wives of the Prophet (PBUH) who said, "He who goes to one who claims to tell about matters of the Unseen and believes in him, his Salat (prayers) will not be accepted for forty days." [Muslim].

The Imam quoted the words of the prophet (PBUH). He tried to make the family see reasons why they shouldn't visit a soothsayer as it was against the teachings of the noble Prophet. However, the family was bent on visiting a soothsayer. They were distressed. They wouldn't mind doing anything in that situation. They discarded the admonitions of the Imam. Grandmother was advised to stay behind because of her age, while Habeebah's parents and Grandmother's brother went to the soothsayer's place.

They journeyed on the road for over an hour before they could get to the soothsayer's house. They got down from the car after completing their journey. It was a village. They walked a short distance through the streets before they located a hut. They stopped in front of the hut. Grandmother's brother knocked on the door. A teenage boy came upon them and asked who they were looking for. "We want to see Baba," Grandmother's brother replied to the boy.

"Baba is not around. He went out for some work," the boy responded, while the family screamed.

"When will he be back?" Grandmother's brother asked anxiously.

"He should be back before 10:00 p.m," the boy replied.

"We will wait for him," the family chorused impatiently.

"Okay, please come inside," the teenage boy told them.

They walked into Baba's house. It was a face-to-face tattered hut. The boy brought a long bench from a room. He placed the bench in the corridor of the house and asked them to sit. They sat impatiently and waited for Baba's return. Even if Baba would return in the middle of the night, they were ready to wait.

CHAPTER SEVEN

Baba did not arrive until past 10:00 p.m, yet Habeebah's family did not leave his house. When Baba got back, the family rushed to him. They didn't allow him to rest before explaining their situation to him. Baba told them not to worry. He ushered them into a room that looked like a shrine. The room was covered with a red cloth. There were candles lit up all over the room. There were also some scary statues in the room. Baba led the way, while Habeebah's family entered.

He made some consultations in front of a white cloth. He shook his head before speaking.

"Your daughter wasn't kidnapped for ransom nor for ritual," Baba said, while the family screamed.

"Then what happened to her?" Habeebah's family asked in unison.

"Be patient, my people. What my god has just revealed to me is that your daughter is a mermaid. Her mermaid family has come to fetch her because her time was up," Baba told them a big lie.

It was obvious he didn't see anything. Habeebah's family screamed. Her mother threw herself on the floor and shouted.

"Baba, please help me. What can I do to bring my daughter back? What can we do to appease the water spirits in order to get my daughter back?" Habeebah's mum asked with teary eyes.

"Baba please, help us," Habeebah's father and Uncle also pleaded. Baba consulted his god again and smiled.

"There's a solution," Baba expressed.

"What's the solution?" Habeebah's family chorused.

"The solution is that the mother of that child will carry a sacrifice to the nearest river by 2:00 a.m to appease the water spirits. After the sacrifice has been accepted. Your daughter will return home. But the sacrifice will cost you money," Baba said.

"We're ready to pay any amount. As long as we can have our daughter back," Habeebah's uncle stated.

"Okay then, the sacrifice will cost you fifty thousand naira because we're going to buy lots of materials to prepare the sacrifice," Baba informed them.

"Fifty thousand naira?" The family exclaimed.

"Yes, fifty thousand naira. Is fifty thousand naira too big to part with in order to save your daughter's life?" Baba asked them.

"No, but please let us pay twenty thousand naira," Habeebah's mum begged him.

"No, if you're not paying fifty thousand naira, then forget about your daughter. This is not a market commodity that you can haggle," Baba expressed bluntly.

"Okay, we'll look for the money," Uncle said, while the family stepped aside to deliberate on how to get the money.

Uncle asked Habeebah's parents how much they had in cash. Habeebah's father replied that he had no money. He told Uncle that he even had to borrow transport fare when he was informed about what happened to his daughter. Habeebah's mum hissed at her ex-husband.

"I know you'll never contribute anything meaningful to this cause because you've always been a useless man," Habeebah's mum insulted her ex-husband, who flared back.

"Don't ever call me useless again you this shrew!" Habeebah's dad responded with an insult.

Uncle shouted at the two of them to keep quiet.

"Will you keep quiet, both of you! Are you supposed to be fighting in this situation? How much do you have, mama Habeebah?" Uncle asked.

"I have seven thousand naira with me," Habeebah's mum replied with tears.

"Bring it," Uncle instructed her.

Habeebah's mum removed the money from the tip of her wrapper where she tied it. She handed it to Uncle. He collected it and spoke to them.

"Someone kept some money with me. I'll go to the nearest ATM to withdraw the money," Uncle said.

"Oh, thank you so much, sir," Habeebah's parents appreciated Uncle in unison.

Uncle informed Baba that he was going to withdraw the money. That locality was a remote area. The nearest ATM stand was some miles away and it was past 11:00 p.m. The money must be given to Baba, without fail, that day because the sacrifice must be done by 2:00 a.m. Uncle and Habeebah's father went to withdraw the money.

They journeyed for an hour to and fro. The road was silent and scary but their mission was important to them. They couldn't back down. They returned to Baba's house at half past 12:00 a.m. Uncle gave Baba a cash of ₦50,000. Baba collected it and began the preparation for the sacrifice.

At exactly 2:00 a.m, Habeebah's mother, escorted by Baba, carried the sacrifice to the nearest river. The sacrifice was placed at the river bank. Baba chanted some incantations. After some minutes, they were done. They returned to Baba's house. Baba told the family that their daughter would have been home before they got home later that morning. The family was happy. They had a little nap in Baba's house before they returned home that morning.

***

After the bike man had left, Habeebah continued crying profusely. She prayed to God to save her from the danger she'd found herself before the next morning. She was really terrified by what the bike man said about killing her the next day and having her organs sold out. She cried and prayed. She begged Allah to have mercy on her. She begged Allah that she doesn't want to die. She begged Allah to save her from the predicament and reunite her with her family.

Habeebah could not tell what time it was but everywhere was dark. She became more afraid with the darkness. She could no longer hear footsteps as she could hear before. She shivered in fear. She could see nothing at all in the darkness. She cried until her eyes were swollen. She was in so much pain that was too much for a little girl of her age to bear. She continued praying non-stop for safety. She didn't know any *adhkar* because she'd never been opportune to learn one. Nonetheless, she prayed in her native language with tears of distress. Mosquitoes dealt terribly with her. And worse still, she couldn't even see them. She couldn't kill them either because her hands had been tied. She thought she could still endure that pain but wouldn't be able to endure a brutal death. She prayed ceaselessly for safety with teary eyes.

Back in Habeebah's house, Grandmother was really worried. She had cried so much. She put a call through to her brother when she didn't see them. Uncle told her they would sleep over and return in the morning as Baba told them a sacrifice had to be done. Uncle assured Grandmother not to worry. He told her Baba assured them that Habeebah would be back in the morning. Grandmother was a little relieved by what Uncle told her. But she couldn't sleep at all till daybreak.

The Imam of the mosque had returned home alongside other sympathisers. After *ishai*, he slept a little and woke up for *tahajjud*. He was really bothered about Habeebah. He wasn't happy with the way her family had gone to seek the help of a soothsayer. He decided to help in his own way; the only way Allah would be pleased with.

The Imam woke up for *tahajjud* and prayed to Allah to save Habeebah. He prayed to Allah to show his greatness to the family. He prayed to Allah to put the soothsayer to shame and open the family's heart to see that the way they sought was nothing but misguidance. The Imam prayed till daybreak. He recited the glorious Quran. He recited a series of *adhkar* for the purpose of protection. He recited the *qunut*. He prayed fervently to Allah to shower His mercy on Habeebah wherever she might be. He prayed to Allah to send His help to her and protect her from any form of danger. The Imam prayed heartily till the *adhan* of *fajr* was called.

***

Mr and Mrs Adesola had abandoned their building for three years because of lack of money. Few weeks ago, Mr Adesola was paid some gratuity from the government. He decided to use that money to complete his abandoned building.

Three days ago, he was in his uncompleted house together with his wife. He discovered that a new lock had been used to lock the gate of his house. He was amazed and feared that his house was about to be snatched. He lodged a complaint to the agent whom he bought his land from. The agent told him he was the one that changed the lock for security reasons. Mr Adesola was relieved of his worry. The agent, who was living in that locality, told him to come for the key of the new lock. Unknown to Mr. Adesola, the agent, in collaboration with kidnappers, were using his uncompleted house as a hideout for their captives.

Unknown to the agent as well, the kidnappers were working behind him in order to cheat him of his own share of any money they realised from their dirty business. The agent didn't know that the kidnappers had Habeebah in captivity in Mr. Adesola's house because he wasn't informed. Because the agent was unaware that the kidnappers had Habeebah in captivity, he didn't bother to call them to ask if the house was free of captives, he just told Mr Adesola to come for the key to his house.

Very early on Tuesday morning, Mr. Adesola set out in his car with his wife. He got to the community by 5:45 a.m. He went to the agent and collected the key to his house. He zoomed off to his house which was in the next street to that of the agent.

From the previous night to the next day, Habeebah had cried a lot. She had nothing to eat nor drink for over 24 hours. She was dehydrated and weak. She couldn't struggle again due to weakness. She couldn't cry anymore as well. However, she wouldn't stop praying ceaselessly for God's protection.

By the time it was 4:00 a.m, she had collapsed and was motionless on the floor. She'd become unconscious.

Mr. Adesola opened the gate of his house and walked round to inspect the compound together with his wife. After inspecting the compound, they walked into the house and checked the room one after the other. When they got to the room Habeebah was tied in, they exclaimed loudly upon seeing a lifeless human on the floor.

Mr. Adesola wanted to touch Habeebah but his wife pulled him back. His wife told him it was dangerous to do so. They didn't know if the person lying motionless was dead or alive. Touching her could implicate them. Mrs. Adesola advised her husband to take photos of Habeebah before doing anything. Mr. Adesola heeded his wife's advice. He took Habeebah's picture, lying motionless, and with her body tied in rope.

The couple were in bewilderment. They wondered how a human being got to their house. And one tied like a goat for that matter.

"Could it be that kidnappers are using my house to hide their captives?" Mr. Adesola marvelled.

"The agent must surely have a hand in this. Please give him a call. Don't mention anything to him. Just tell him to come here," Mrs. Adesola advised her husband.

Mr. Adesola picked his phone and put a call across to the agent. He told him he wanted to entrust his house project to him. The agent came running at the mention of the house project.

When the agent arrived, Mr. Adesola showed Habeebah's motionless body to him. Without mincing words, Mr. Adesola accused the agent of being a kidnapper or a kidnapper accomplice because he was the only one who had the key to his house.

The agent tried to lie but Mr. Adesola gave him a dirty slap. Mr. Adesola thought the best way was to inform the police. The police were informed. Some representatives of the Nigerian force were sent to check out the crime scene. When the police arrived, they moved over to Habeebah and discovered that she was still breathing. They tried to wake her up but she wasn't responding. They called for an ambulance that would convey her to the hospital.

The agent was interrogated and later arrested. He was whisked to the police station. The police tortured him to disclose his partners. He disclosed the name of the bike man and others. The police arrested them all. They would be tried in a court of law for kidnapping and attempted murder.

At the hospital, Habeebah was attended to immediately. The doctors were able to revive her. They set the line for her to get some drip. She was responding to treatment but was still unconscious. The police would wait for her to regain consciousness. After which she would be asked questions concerning her family.

Back in Habeebah's house, Habeebah's parents and Uncle had returned home from the soothsayer's house. The soothsayer assured them that they would meet Habeebah at home but they didn't. Grandmother shouted and wailed when Habeebah didn't return that morning. Habeebah's parents and Uncle were disappointed. They consoled the rest of the family that they should keep on hoping for Habeebah's return, as Baba had assured them.

The Imam of their community mosque arrived in the morning to check on the family. He assured the family not to panic that Habeebah would be back. The Imam advised them to go back to the police to lodge a complaint as 24 hours had already passed. Habeebah's uncle objected to the Imam's advice. He said Habeebah would be back that morning because he had faith in the soothsayer. The Imam cautioned him not to have faith in humans, but Allah.

It was noon already and Habeebah was not back. At this juncture, it dawned on the family that the soothsayer was nothing but a liar. He doesn't have the power to see the future or what it holds. As a matter of fact, no one had the power to see the future except Allah. When the situation was getting out of hand, the family started calling upon Allah. They were ready to run to Allah, as no one could save except Him. Uncle was ready to listen to the Imam's advice. Uncle, Habeebah's father and the Imam went to the police station to lodge a complaint about the missing Habeebah. When they got to the police station, they informed the police about their missing daughter.

The time they got to the station coincided with the time the bike man, the house agent and their accomplices were brought down from the police van. They'd been transferred from another police station to that particular one.

The police pushed them into the station ferociously like criminals that they were. Habeebah's father asked a Policeman about the crime they committed. He was told they kidnapped a little girl. At the mention of a little girl, Habeebah's father started bombarding the Policeman with questions, anxiously.

"Has the girl been rescued from them? Where is the girl that they kidnapped? Is she still alive? Can I see her? She could be my daughter, the one that had gone missing since yesterday," Habeebah's father asked restlessly.

The Imam and Uncle also reiterated what he had said.

"Yes please, let us see the girl that was kidnapped, she could be the one we're looking for," the Imam and Uncle expressed in unison.

The Policeman told them that the girl had been admitted to a hospital because she was found unconscious. Habeebah's father screamed again.

"Is my daughter still alive?" Habeebah's father exclaimed.

The Policeman told him to calm down.

"Please be patient. The girl is still alive. But we ain't sure if she's your daughter or not………," The Policeman was trying to explain, but Habeebah's father interrupted him.

"Please, let us see her. The only way to know if she's the one we're looking for or not is to see her. Isn't it Uncle?" Habeebah's father asked Grandmother's brother, who nodded his head in agreement.

"Yes, that's true. The only way to know the identity of the child in the hospital is to see her," Uncle concurred.

The Policeman agreed to their request. Another Policeman was appointed to go with them to the hospital.

They journeyed to the hospital for another 30 minutes. Habeebah's father rushed into the hospital. He was anxious to see his daughter. Even though he wasn't sure the girl on admission would be his daughter, he was optimistic. The Policeman led the way into the ward Habeebah was admitted in.

They opened the door and moved closer to Habeebah who was still unconscious. Upon sighting Habeebah, her father screamed loudly.

"She's my daughter! She's my daughter!! She's my daughter!!!" Habeebah's father exclaimed repeatedly with tears of joy.

The Imam was dazed. He was amazed at the mercy and greatness of Allah. Uncle was diggy. Finding Habeebah in a hospital had proved the soothsayer wrong. He was nothing but a scammer. A dubious fraudster who was just looking for his daily bread. Uncle could not believe that he was scammed. The saddest thing was that the money doesn't even belong to him; he borrowed it. He saved his grief for another time. As for now, the family must jubilate and thank Allah for protecting Habeebah and reuniting her with them.

Habeebah's father asked the nurse when Habeebah would wake up. The nurse replied that she would wake up anytime soon. The words of the nurse relieved him of his tension. He brought out his phone to share the good news that Habeebah had been found with the rest of the family.

CHAPTER EIGHT

Habeebah woke up later that evening. Her father shouted happily after she woke up. He moved closer to her and embraced her tightly. He chanted *Alhamdulillah* countlessly. He kissed her forehead affectionately. Habeebah was confused at first. She didn't know where she was. But after seeing her father and Uncle clearly, she knew she must have been in a safe place.

"How are you Habeebah?" Habeebah's father asked with mixed feelings; excitement and worry.

"I'm hungry," Habeebah said instead of replying to her father's question.

Habeebah's father quickly went out of the ward to call a nurse. He informed the nurse that Habeebah had woken up and that she was hungry. The nurse followed him to examine her. After the examination, the nurse told Habeebah's father to get her something to eat. He rushed out to get food for his daughter.

After Habeebah had finished eating, she felt an indescribable ease from within.

"Thank you my dear daughter for surviving. What happened to you exactly?" Habeebah's father asked her.

Habeebah explained how she was kidnapped by the bike man. And how she was tied and starved for 24 hours. Her family screamed loudly.

"People are wicked," the Imam exclaimed. "How can they treat a little girl so inhumanely?" The Imam asked a rhetorical question.

"People are wicked, indeed," Uncle expressed. "We just thank God that we didn't have any cause to mourn over Habeebah. We praise Him and adore Him. He has done something marvellous for us," Uncle was thankful to Allah.

"You'll never hawk again," Habeebah's father said. "In fact, I'm taking you with me when I'm leaving. I won't allow you to live with Grandmother again," Habeebah's father said.

Habeebah objected.

"No, daddy, I can't go with you. Do you remember the time I came to your place with my sibling to spend the holiday? You would leave us in the house all by ourselves for days without coming home to sleep. The day you'll come home, you'll always return drunk to stupor. Let me continue to live with my grandmother," Habeebah said.

Her father felt guilty for failing in his responsibility as a father.

Uncle turned to Habeebah's father and cleared his throat before speaking.

"Habeebah will continue to live with my sister because I can't entrust her to you. You have proven to be an irresponsible father. She'll stop hawking by the grace of God. And I want to implore you to start sending alimony to Grandmother every month, so that what has happened will never repeat itself. You can't abandon your children with an old woman and not look back. What do you think, Imam?" Uncle asked, inviting Imam to the conversation.

"Yes, it is true. A father should always stand up to his responsibility. The prophet (PBUH) said: *"Every one of you is a shepherd and is responsible for his flock. The leader of the people is a guardian and is responsible for his subjects. A man is the guardian of his family and he is responsible for them……"* From the little you are earning, always put your family's needs at the top list of your priority. May Allah enrich your pocket," the Imam supplicated, to which Uncle and Habeebah's father responded with 'Aamin'.

After a while, Uncle asked the Imam if Allah was going to forgive them for going to a soothsayer, and if Allah would accept their prayers for 40 days as stated in the hadith of the prophet, (PBUH). The Imam replied to them to ask for Allah's forgiveness sincerely and never do such a thing again as Allah is GAFURU-R-RAHEEM. The Imam told them to continue observing their five daily prayers while seeking Allah's repentance and hoping that He would forgive them and accept their prayers. "Although, the only sin Allah does not forgive is associating partners with Him, and visiting a soothsayer is associating partners with Allah. However, a living person still has the grace of seeking repentance. Only a dead person can no longer seek repentance," The Imam replied sagely.

After the Imam had answered his questions, Uncle asked another question. He asked the Imam to teach them the *adhkar* of protection.

The Imam taught them a number of *adhkar* for general protection. He told them they could get a copy of 'citadel of the believer' to have unlimited access to the *adhkar*. Part of the adhkar the Imam taught the family were:

'Bismillahil-lazi la yadhurru ma'asmihi syai'un fil ardhi wa la fis-sama'i wa huwas-sami'ul aleem'

'In the Name of Allah with Whose Name there is protection against every kind of harm in the earth or in heaven, and He is All-Hearing and All-Knowing'

'Allahumma inni as'alukal-'afwa wal 'afiyah fid-dunya wal-akhirah'

'O Allah, I seek Your forgiveness and my well-being in this world and the Hereafter'

'Allahummah-fazni min baini yadaiya, wa min khalfi, wa 'an yameeni, wa 'an shimali wa min fauqi, wa audhu bi'azamatika an ughtala min tahti'

'O Allah protect me from my front, behind me, from my right and my left, and from above me, and I seek refuge in Your Magnificence from being taken unaware from beneath me'

'A'uzu bikalimatillahit-tammati min sharri ma khalaq'

'I seek protection in the perfect words of Allah from every evil that has been created'

'Allahumma inni a'uzubika minal baras, wal junuun wal juzzam, wa min sayyi'il-asqam'

'O Allah, I seek refuge in You from leprosy, madness, elephantiasis, and evil diseases'.

Lastly, the Imam taught them the *adhkar* to chant before leaving the house.

'Bismillahi tawakkaltu alallahi la hawla wala quwwata illa billah'

'In the name of Allah, I trust in Allah; there is no might and no power but in Allah'

The Imam qouted the *Hadith* of the prophet that explained the prayer to say before leaving the house. Narrated Anas ibn Malik, The Prophet (PBUH) said: *When a man goes out of his house and says: "In the name of Allah, I trust in Allah; there is no might and no power but in Allah," the following will be said to him at that time: "You are guided, defended and protected." The devils will go far from him and another devil will say: How can you deal with a man who has been guided, defended and protected?"* The Imam quoted.

Uncle and Habeebah's father were grateful to the Imam. Uncle implored Habeebah to be chanting the *adhkar* constantly. Uncle also told the Imam that he would like Habeebah and the other grandchildren to start attending the *madrasah* in his mosque. The Imam said he would be so glad to have the children in his *madrasah*.

That evening, Habeebah's mother and Grandmother visited the hospital with food. It was a happy reunion for both the grandchild and her grandmother. Habeebah's mother shed tears of joy. She was happy that her daughter was found. She couldn't stop staring amazingly at Habeebah. She was so scared when Habeebah was missing. She thought she had lost a daughter.

Grandmother could not have enough of Habeebah. She doted on her. She was all over her with kisses and cuddling. She checked all her body thoroughly for any sign of bruises. The parts of her body where she was tied up were seriously bruised. The mosquito bites also left a sore on her body.

Grandmother told her sorry over and over again. Grandmother couldn't stop thanking Allah for bringing Habeebah safely to her. She raised her palms up and thanked Allah for His mercies.

"*Alhamdulillah Rabil'aalamin*. Thank you Allah for protecting my grandchild from the evil that nearly befell her. Thank you for saving my family from mourning. Forgive us for not relying on you. Forgive us for seeking your creature's help," Grandmother expressed her utmost gratitude to Allah.

She turned to Habeebah and spoke nicely to her.

"Sorry my darling. You'll never hawk again. I'll never allow you to hawk again. We will be eating whatever we see. You're much more precious to me than money. In fact, if it's not yet daybreak and the lines on the palm are not clearly seen, I will never allow any of you to step out again. No more hawking," Grandmother said, while Habeebah's mother chimed in.

"Yes, I agree. She should not hawk again. If only her father had been a responsible man, we would not have found ourselves in this situation. But no problem, henceforth, I'll endeavour to send money to you every month, no matter how small," Habeebah's mum pledged, while Grandma prayed for her.

***

The next day, which was Wednesday, Habeebah was discharged from the hospital. Her parents took her home. The neighbours were excited to see her. In fact, the whole community was extremely elated to see her. It was a beautiful reunion.

In her school, the students and teachers were worried that Habeebah had not been in school since Monday. Her class teacher asked her colleagues if anyone knew her house to which they replied in the negative. The school didn't take it so seriously on Monday and Tuesday. But when Habeebah didn't show up on Wednesday as well, her class teacher knew something must be wrong.

The class teacher went to check the school records and found the mobile number of Habeebah's father. On Wednesday afternoon, the teacher put a call across to Habeebah's father. Since Habeebah had been found on Tuesday evening, her father didn't mention to the teacher that she was kidnapped. He just told her that she was sick and that she would be in school by the coming week.

When Habeebah heard what her dad said over the phone, she shook her head and told her father that the coming week was too far away. She told her father that she must be in school the next day. The Mathematics competition would be held the following Monday and she'd been chosen among the school representatives. Her family told her to rest well before she resumed school activities but she objected convincingly. She made them see reasons she had to participate in the competition. After several back and forths, her family agreed that she resumed school the next day, which was Thursday, on the condition that she would not leave home until 7:00 a.m.

The following day, Habeebah went to school. She couldn't attend the preparatory-class which started by 7:00 a.m. Her colleagues were happy and surprised to see her back in school that day. The class teacher had told them that she was indisposed and wouldn't be in school until the following week. Her colleagues told her that the school was planning to send representatives to her house to pay her a courtesy visit. But seeing her in school that day, both her colleagues and teachers were happy.

Mr. Ige, the Mathematics teacher, rescheduled the time of the competition-preparatory-class till close of school because Habeebah told him she wouldn't be able to make it in the morning because of her health. She didn't tell anyone she was kidnapped, as instructed by her family. Her family feared that she might be mocked by her schoolmates if she told them what happened, hence, they warned her never to tell anyone that she was kidnapped.

The English teacher, Mrs. Babalola, was in their classroom on Thursday afternoon to teach them English Language. As she was teaching them, she noticed some marks on Habeebah's wrist. The mark she got from the rope the kidnappers used in tying her. The teacher asked Habeebah to see her during the lunch break.

During the lunch break, Habeebah went to see the English teacher. The teacher asked her to sit down. She sat and wondered why the teacher had summoned her.

"What happened to your wrist?" The teacher asked with concern, while pointing at her wrist.

Habeebah quickly hid her wrist behind her back. The teacher smiled.

"You can tell me anything. I'm asking you not as your teacher, but as your mother. What happened to your wrist? The mark was not there before. Are you being mistreated at home?" The teacher asked.

Habeebah shook her head.

"No, ma."

"Did you fight with anyone?" The teacher pestered her.

"No, ma."

"Then, how did you get the mark on your wrist?" The teacher insisted on knowing.

"Errrrmm…….Errrrmmmm….," Habeebah stuttered.

"Relax, my dear. You can trust me. I won't tell anyone," The teacher assured her.

"I was kidnapped on Monday morning, ma."

"*Subhana'llah*!" The teacher exclaimed.

"Yes, ma. I was tied like a goat. The mark is the one I sustained from the rope, ma."

"*Eeya*, I'm so sorry, my darling. How did it happen?" Mrs. Babalola pestered.

"I used to hawk for my grandmother everyday before I came to school. And because of the competition-preparatory-class that was slated for 7:00 a.m everyday, I changed the time of my hawking to 5:15 a.m."

"5:15 a.m? Oh my goodness! That was too early."

"Yes, ma. I was hawking that Monday morning when the kidnapper barricaded me. He told me he wanted to buy some pap. That was the last thing I knew until I woke up in an uncompleted building."

"Oh my God! I'm so sorry to hear that. May God's protection never cease upon you. I understand the situation at home must have been so bad before your grandmother could push you out so early to hawk. We live in a dangerous world where human lives are not valued. Parents must be very vigilant. Parents must protect their children from all harm; and hawking inclusive. Hawking can be very dangerous, especially for little children. I'm so sorry to hear about your experience, darling," Mrs. Babalola sympathised with Habeebah.

"Thank you, ma." Habeebah replied with gratitude.

"Please don't allow the experience to affect you. You're brilliant. You're beautiful. You're bold. You're brave. You're destined for greatness. No harm shall befall you by the mercy of Allah. Don't worry, my dear, you'll get over the experience with time," Mrs. Babalola instilled some self confidence in Habeebah.

"Thank you so much, ma."

"You're welcome, my darling. Henceforth, you are free to come to me for anything you need, okay!" Mrs Babalola offered to help.

"Yes, ma. I'll do that, ma. I'm very grateful to you, ma," Habeebah appreciated Mrs. Babalola, who dismissed her afterwards.

After that day, Mrs. Babalola kept to her words. She made sure she gave Habeebah money everyday; as a way of assisting her in her own little way.

***

On the day of the competition, Khadijah, Hamzah and Habeebah got to school early. The school bus conveyed them to the competition alongside their Mathematics teacher, Mr. Ige.

The competition was an oral one. The total number of schools that participated in the competition were fifteen. Students were asked to pick numbers for their questions. The three schools that performed above average were picked for the final. Of which, Kings and Queens College was among. The final round of the competition lasted for the next 30 minutes.

The winner was announced after the collation of results. And the winner was Kings and Queens College. The hall went into a galore of screaming after the winner was announced. The school was showered with accolades. The students were celebrated for their hard work and exceptional performances.

A star prize of a digital printer and a desktop computer were awarded to the school. While a cash prize of ₦150,000 was awarded to the representatives. A prize of ₦50,000 was also given to Mr. Ige, the Mathematics teacher, for tutoring the students to success.

It was a joyous day for the students, as well as their teacher. The school had already closed before they returned that day. The following day at the assembly, the principal called upon the trio of Khadijah, Habeebah and Hamzah to the podium. Their mathematics teacher was also called to the podium.

The star prize was displayed for all to see. The principal announced the good news excitedly.

"I'm happy to inform you that our school emerged as the overall winner in the mathematics competition that was held yesterday," the principal announced.

The school screamed joyously.

"Yes, our students, in persons of Khadijah, Hamzah and Habeebah, who represented the school in the Mathematics competition, made it possible for the school to emerge as the overall winner of the competition. They made the school proud. They made their parents proud. And they've also made themselves proud. We are proud of them. This digital printer and desktop computer are the prizes they won for the school. They also won a cash prize of ₦50,000 for themselves each. Also, Mr. Ige, their Mathematics teacher, has also been rewarded with ₦50,000," the principal announced proudly, while the other students and teachers hailed the exceptional students and their teacher.

The principal went further to encourage other students to also work hard so that they could be celebrated like Khadijah, Habeebah and Hamzah. The three of them held their heads high as they were showered with ovations from both students and teachers.

Mrs. Babalola specially congratulated Habeebah for performing up to expectation despite the horrible experience she went through before the competition.

"I am proud of you, Habeebah. I am happy that you didn't allow the bad experience that you had, to blight your success. Go girl! The sky is your starting point," Mrs. Babalola encouraged Habeebah with smiles.

CHAPTER NINE

Khadijah's parents were proud of her. The school sent her ₦50,000 cash prize to her father's account. Her parents praised her for a job well done. They encouraged her never to relent.

"I'm proud of you, my baby girl," her mother said to her with a grin.

"Thank you, mummy," she replied to her mum with smiles.

"I'm very proud of you, Khadijah. I've always known that my daughter is outstanding. Now I am more certain that she is super-duper astounding," her father praised her, while she blushed.

"What do you want to do with your money?" Chief Oniru asked his daughter.

"I don't know. I don't really need it. You and mum have been so amazing. I do not lack anything. So, I don't know what to do with the money," Khadijah replied, but quickly shook her head before her parents could respond.

"I think I know what to do with the money," Khadijah said sharply.

"What?" Her parents chorused.

"I'll donate it to the orphanage," she replied sensibly.

Her parents exchanged glances. They grinned proudly.

Her mother pulled her to her embrace.

"Oh my darling, you're so sweet with a beautiful soul," her mother said with emotions.

Her father stroked her hair fondly.

"I'm proud of you, my darling. Keep it up. You have a good heart. Your wish shall be respected. We'll donate the money to the orphanage on your behalf," her father assured her.

"Thank you so much, daddy and mummy. You made it so easy for me to think about others. Thanks for giving me the wings to fly," Khadijah appreciated her parents with smiles.

***

Habeebah, on the other hand, returned home and informed her grandmother of the ₦50,000 cash prize.

She narrated to her family in excitement, how her school won the mathematics competition. And how each representative was given ₦50,000 each. Grandmother asked about the money but Habeebah said the school didn't give the money to her but told her to invite her grandmother to school to receive the money on her behalf.

The following day, Grandmother went to the school around noon. Since she didn't have an account with any bank, the principal decided to give her the money in cash. Grandmother received the ₦50,000 cash prize on behalf of Habeebah. She was thankful to the principal. She walked out of the principal's office with smiles.

The time Grandmother walked out of the principal's office coincided with the close of school for the day. Grandmother went to fetch Habeebah in her class. Habeebah jumped on her happily. Grandmother showed the money to Habeebah in excitement. They returned home together.

When they got home, they met a visitor; Grandmother's brother. Grandmother excitedly narrated to her brother, how Habeebah won a cash prize of ₦50,000 in her school competition. She brought out the money from her bag and proudly showed it to her brother. To her dismay, her brother quickly snatched the money from her.

"Let me have the money," Uncle said, while snatching the money from Grandmother.

Grandmother and Habeebah were confused. A lot of questions were written all over their faces. Uncle nodded his head before speaking.

"Yes, I should be the one to have the money. Do you remember the ₦50,000 I gave the soothsayer? I borrowed the money from a friend and he's been on my neck to return the money. This Mathematics cash prize has come at the right time. Habeebah, well done, we're very proud of you. Keep it up, okay!" Uncle said and left the room.

Tears welled up in Habeebah's eyes. She had thought that she would give the money to Grandmother to start a petty business outside the house. She had a lot of needs as well which she would have loved to fulfill with part of the money. But the money was sadly gone.

"Don't worry, my darling," Grandmother placated her. "Money is nothing as long as you're here with me, hale and hearty," Grandmother said.

"No, Grandma, money is a lot. Since the day I got discharged from the hospital, we've not received any monetary assistance from anyone. Even my daddy that promised to be sending money henceforth has not sent a dime. Since the day my mummy left as well, we haven't heard from her. The Imam of our community mosque was the only one that brought food stuff for us two days after I was discharged from the hospital. May Allah bless him. And Mrs. Babalola, my English teacher, has been responsible for my transport fare since the day she knew about my story. Now that she knows that I received ₦50,000, will she still continue to give me money? Grandmother, we can't continue to live like this. We can't," Habeebah said with excruciating pain.

Her grandmother embraced and consoled her.

"Don't cry, my darling. We will not continue to live like this. Allah will send a helper to us very soon," Grandmother assured her.

"I hope so. I just hope so."

"Thank you for understanding the situation. May God bless you immensely," Grandmother prayed for her.

"Amin. Hmmmmmmmmmmm," Habeebah breathed heavily. She quickly discarded her worry. She could perceive the aroma of her grandmother's signature stew.

"I can smell something nice. What did you cook, Grandmother? I am hungry," Habeebah said, while sniffing so hard.

"I made some rice with stew," Grandmother replied, while Habeebah grinned.

She hurried to the kitchen to get the food.

Hamzah Bello's cash prize was also sent to his father's account. His family was happy and proud of him. His father carried him up proudly with showers of eulogy. Hamzah smiled proudly. He was delighted to have made his parents happy.

***

In the next English Language class, Mrs. Babalola, the English teacher, taught them an argumentative essay. During the lesson, Suwebah wasn't concentrating. She was busy sulking, while the lesson was going on. The teacher moved closer to her and asked her what the problem was.

"Suwebah, what is the matter with you? Your mind is not in the class," The teacher asked, while Suwebah replied that nothing was wrong with her.

"Come on! Don't give me that! I know something is wrong. Why will you be absent-minded in the class if nothing is wrong? Now tell me whatever it is that is bothering you," Mrs. Babalola urged her. At this time, Suwebah opened up.

"I wanted a new school shoe but my mum didn't buy it for me," Suwebah replied.

The class laughed.

"Keep quiet, all of you," the teacher instructed the class and then turned to Suwebah. "You want a new school shoe and that's why you've been sulking? Don't you have any before?" The teacher asked her.

"I have," Suwebah replied.

"How many do you have?" Mrs. Babalola asked.

"I have four," Suwebah replied, while Abbas passed a jibe at her.

"When you're crying that you have no shoes, what should people who have no legs do?" Abbas said jokingly, while the teacher cautioned him.

"Abbas is right. I asked him to keep quiet because I didn't ask him to speak. Now listen to me children! Always be content with whatever you have. Always be content with whatever your parents are able to provide for you. Thank Allah for providing for your parents. Be grateful to your parents for catering for your needs. Lack of contentment is the first step towards ingratitude. Lack of contentment is a step towards theft," Mrs. Babalola admonished the students.

"Thank you, ma," the students chorused.

"In addition, always pray for your parents. Pray that Allah should provide for them so that they can cater for your needs. Be grateful for the little that you have. Some children don't have any at all. Some children are so needy that as young as they are, they know what it means to survive because they struggle for their daily bread. Some needy children are going through a lot. Some children are not as privileged as you are, yet you cannot know because they don't carry their problems on their faces. They remain cheerful even in the face of adversity. Please be grateful for the little you have. Gratitude will always make you reflect. And you'll never sulk whenever you can't get what you want."

"What if we need that thing badly? We'll surely sulk if we can't get it," Rasheed said, while the teacher shook her head before responding.

"Want is different from need. Needs are the essential things you need for survival. While want is just what you desire. They are not attached to your survival. You probably just want them for pleasure. For your age, what you really need now are food, clothing, shelter, education and school necessities such as a school bag, school books, school shoes and other necessities. And if your parents are able to provide just one each, out of the aforementioned things, then be grateful. Any addition is just what you desire which is not necessary. I hope you understand," Mrs. Babalola expressed.

The students chorused a yes answer.

All the while Mrs. Babalola was speaking, she was reflecting on Habeebah's story. She wished her classmates knew her story. She wished they were aware of her struggles, then they would be grateful for the little their parents were able to provide for them.

While speaking to the students, something struck the teacher. She smiled. She decided to use what she'd admonished the students about as a topic for their debate which they would take home as their homework.

After the lesson, she wrote the topic on the board. 'Wealthy children are more privileged than the needy children.' She told the girls they would support, while the boys were to debate against the topic. The assignment would be submitted the next day in the morning, while the teacher would go through them. And the best two debates would be read in the class.

The students went home with the homework. They all racked their brains to come up with a beautiful debate. Some students sought the assistance of their parents. Some of them sought the assistance of their older siblings. They all did the assignment and submitted it to Mrs. Babalola's table the next day.

During the English Language lesson later that day, Mrs. Babalola came to class with the students' notebooks.

She taught them briefly and then announced the best two debates. Anat Omotosho had the best debate for the supporting category, while Hamzah Bello had the best debate for the opposing category.

The teacher read out the two best debates. She started from Anat's own which supported the motion.

'The topic of the debate is **'Wealthy children are more privileged than the needy children.' What is privilege? Privilege is an advantage some set of people have over others. The wealthy children are children whose parents are well off. The wealthy children are more privileged than the needy children in a number of ways. Wealthy children have good houses over their heads. Wealthy children have good food to eat. Wealthy children have good clothes to wear. Wealthy children attend good schools. Wealthy children have access to good healthcare. Wealthy children have access to amusement and pleasures. Wealthy children perform well in school because they do not have to worry about anything. They do not lack anything, therefore, they divert all their attention to their studies. In contrast to this, needy children are lacking in a number of ways. Needy children don't have good houses to live in. Some of them don't even have houses at all. They roam the street in tattered clothes, while begging for alms. Because they don't have a roof over their heads, they are prone to mosquito bites which causes malaria. Needy children are prone to assault because they are street children and the street is dangerous. Needy children don't have good food to eat. Most of the time, they go to bed hungry or suffer malnutrition.**

Needy children don't have good clothes to wear. They always appear unkempt in tattered clothes. Needy children are prone to diseases due to their poor basic hygiene, yet they do not have access to healthcare. Needy children are also prone to stealing, hooliganism and promiscuity. When they cannot endure hunger, they'll steal to feed themselves. When they can't afford basic necessities of life, the girls among them may become wayward; using what they have to get what they want. And because they grow up in the street with little or no guidance from parents, the boys among them may turn into hoodlums who pose a threat to the peace of the society. The needy children will not perform well in school because they have so many distractions and so many inconveniences. The government has a role to play in seeing that street children are being catered for. The government should provide more jobs so that parents can have adequate resources to raise their children. The government should build low cost houses that poor masses can afford. The government should provide basic amenities like water, electricity, healthcare facilities so that the poor masses can benefit. The government should also provide free education at all levels. The government should also equip farmers with adequate tools and resources so that food can be cheap for all to get. With these few points of mine, I hope I have been able to convince you that wealthy children are more privileged than the needy children.'

The teacher concluded Anat's debate, while the class cheered. Mrs. Babalola spoke afterwards.

"Almost every one of you raised very good points. Why I chose Anat's debate as the best is that she postulated solutions to the problems of the needy children. And that was why she scored more points. The second debate is that of Hamzah Bello. He opposed the motion tactically and I'm so proud of him," the teacher said and began to read Hamzah's debate.

'My name is Hamzah Bello, and I want to oppose the motion which says: Wealthy children are more privileged than the needy children. Wealthy children are not more privileged than the needy children. It is true that needy children go through life challenges but without challenges, some life lessons won't be learnt. Challenges prepare us for bigger things in life. Challenges teach us to be resilient. Challenges teach us to never give up on our dreams. The needy children are rather more privileged than the wealthy children because they grow up with a formidable strength which makes them conquer any test in life. Unlike the wealthy children who have everything on a platter of gold, the needy children struggle for every bread they eat; therefore, they know the importance of survival. If we put a wealthy child and a needy child in a dark tunnel, i.e, a difficult situation, the needy child is likely to survive because of the resilient spirit he's learnt in the cause of his survival, while the wealthy child is more likely to fall by the wayside because he's always had the support of his wealthy parents, he's never really been independent, he doesn't know what it is like to struggle for survival, therefore, challenges will be strange to him. He might not be able to handle it. In addition, needy children are found to be more exposed than the wealthy children. They've struggled for survival all their life; so they know the nitty-gritty of the environment around them. It will be difficult for them to be harmed, while the wealthy children can be susceptible and vulnerable to harm and the evil of men because of their lack of exposure. Furthermore, the needy child turns out to be a hard worker who never relents because there's no one to support him to succeed. He always would

climb the ladder of success to the finish line. He'd been equipped with adequate doggedness to always fight difficulty, he would never back down until he's reached the promised land. Unlike the wealthy child who has been dependent on his parents all his life, any little challenge will sway him and completely put him off track. Moreover, the needy child is independent. He believes in himself. He doesn't need anyone's validation to boost his self-confidence. That self-confidence has always been his most treasured weapon, anyway. The needy child only has himself, therefore, he braces up and conquers the world with determination. He's independent in thoughts and actions. He knows very well that no one has left any wealth for him, so he works hard relentlessly to achieve his own wealth, no matter how long it may take. The wealthy child, on the other hand, depends on his parents, 99%. He needs his parents' validation before he could carry on with any decision. He's not independent in thoughts and actions, his parents always decide for him. He knows he's been left with a lot of bounty, so he relaxes and never bothers to make his own money. Some wealthy children become so lazy. And worse still, squanderous. They spend their parents' wealth lavishly on frivolities. Because they never sweat to get money, they become wasteful. Unlike the needy child who spends prudently because he sweats to get every penny. And lastly, wealthy or needy, the most important thing is happiness. Happiness is free. Happiness can't be bought with money. There are lots of wealthy people who ain't happy. And there are numerous needy people who find happiness in gratitude. Happiness is gratitude. Gratitude to God Almighty is happiness. With these few points of mine, I hope I've been able to convince you that wealthy children are not more privileged than the needy ones.'

The teacher concluded Hamzah's debate, while the other students cheered. Abbas and the other students hailed Hamzah.

"Hamzah! *Papapa*! Hamzah! *Papapa*! Hamzah! *Papapa*!" Abbas hailed him, while the other students joined him.

The teacher left them to display their happiness. After a while, she asked them to stop.

"That's enough. You have all tried. Your debates are thought-provoking and educating. Anat's debate wins the supporting category, while Hamzah's debate wins the opposing category. I have a prize for the two of them," the teacher announced, while the class exclaimed happily.

"I said, I have a prize for Hamzah and Anat and not all of you, why are you all excited?" The teacher asked, Abbas quickly responded.

"We're happy because victory to one is victory to all, ma." Abbas replied with smiles.

"That's very good. I love your spirit of solidarity, Abbas. Keep it up. The prize I have for Hamzah and Anat is a dictionary each…," the teacher announced, the class exclaimed again.

The teacher cautioned them to allow her to talk.

"The dictionary is used for checking the meaning of words. The rest of you can get it as well," the teacher encouraged them.

Khadijah and some other students replied to the teacher that they had it already.

The teacher left the class after telling Habeebah to see her during the lunch break.

Habeebah went to see Mrs. Babalola during the lunch break. The teacher asked her to sit in front of her.

"Did you listen to Hamzah's debate?" Mrs Babalola asked her.

"Yes, ma," Habeebah replied.

"What did you learn from it?" Mrs. Babalola asked her again.

"I learnt that I should never give up. I should continue racing for success till I get to the finish line. I learnt that no matter my background, I should never lose focus. I learnt that happy people are grateful people," Habeebah recounted what she'd learnt.

Mrs. Babalola was proud of her.

"I'm very proud of you, my darling. Anywhere you may find yourself and in any situation, know that you're destined for greatness and never give up on your dreams. Continue to race for success and encourage yourself, even if I'm no longer here to motivate you," Mrs Babalola advised her.

Her last statement hit Habeebah.

"Even if you're no longer here? What do you mean, ma?" Habeebah asked.

"My dear, I am relocating to the United States to be with my husband by the end of this term," Mrs. Babalola dropped the bomb shell.

Habeebah exclaimed and cried.

She quickly got up from her seat and went to give Mrs. Babalola a hug.

"Oh my sweet teacher, why should you leave me at this time? I'll miss you so much," Habeebah said with witty eyes.

"Oh my darling, I'll miss you too. But don't forget all I've told you. Never stop racing to success until you get to the finish line. Don't ever give up. Don't allow the kind of background you come from to blight your bright future, okay!" Mrs. Babalola motivated Habeebah.

"Yes, ma. I'll act on your advice. Thank you, ma. I'll miss you so much."

"I'll miss you too, my darling. And I'll also give you a copy of the same dictionary that I'm giving to Hamzah and Anat."

"*Yaaaayyyyyy*!" Habeebah jubilated. "Thank you, ma."

"You're most welcome, my darling."

CHAPTER TEN

The first term examination arrived after 12 weeks of serious academic term. On the last day of school, the students collected their report cards. The students of JSS1A were seen comparing their results. Khadijah Oniru topped the class with the first position. Habeebah Adetola followed closely with the second position. Hamzah Bello had the third position. The other members of the class were not surprised at the performances of the three. They'd always proven themselves to be exceptionally brilliant.

The fourth position was taken by Anat Omotosho. All the students jubilated because they all performed excellently.

Khadijah was very excited. She felt on top of the world. She'd always had the first position right from primary school. She was so happy that she was able to maintain a good record even in secondary school.

As soon as her mum arrived to take her home, she broke the news of her first position to her excitedly. Her mum hugged and kissed her passionately. Mrs. Oniru felt so proud of her daughter. She felt fulfilled as a mother. She always loved her daughter to be the first among her peers. And that wish had always been fruitful. She couldn't be more grateful.

Mrs. Oniru put a call through to the house. She instructed the cook to prepare a special delicacy for Khadijah. As soon as mother and daughter got home, they were welcomed by the aroma of fried rice and roasted chicken. Khadijah ate her fill.

When her dad returned in the evening, he presented a box of gifts to Khadijah. When she unwrapped the gift, she found an iPad and a set of stationary. She screamed loudly in excitement. She rushed to give her dad a hug.

"Thank you so much, daddy. I love the gift so much," Khadijah said excitedly.

"You're welcome, my darling. I am so proud of you. Continue to make me proud and I'll continue to shower you with gifts," Chief Oniru replied.

"I promise to always make you proud. I shall work hard to cling on to the first position throughout my secondary education," Khadijah promised radiantly.

"That's my girl! And I'll continue to hold you in high esteem," Chief Oniru replied.

It was a beautiful atmosphere to behold as Khadijah's parents doted on her, while she basked in the euphoria of the pleasant ambience.

The last day of the term was also Mrs. Babalola's last day in school. She was relocating to the U.S.A. to be with her husband. Habeebah ran to her office after collecting her report card. Mrs. Babalola hugged her affectionately.

"I am so proud of you, my darling. The sky is your starting point. Despite the challenges you're faced with, you still managed to secure the second position out of tens of students in your class. I am extremely proud of you. Your strength will never dwindle unless you relax. Keep aiming high because you're destined for greatness. And never allow your background to affect your focus. Don't be distracted. Continue to push harder and you'll excel in the end," Mrs. Babalola motivated Habeebah over again.

"Thank you for your unrelenting words of encouragement, ma. I'll miss you so much," Habeebah said with a sad face.

Mrs. Babalola fondled her cheeks.

"Come on sweetheart! Don't give me that face. Whether I'm around or not, I trust that you'll never look back but keep climbing till you reach the rooftop, isn't it?"

"Yes, ma."

"That's my girl!" Mrs. Babalola cheered Habeebah.

They bade themselves goodbye. Habeebah would miss her. The next academic term would be boring without her, certainly.

Habeebah got home and showed her brilliant result to her grandmother. Grandmother was excited. She hugged Habeebah and prayed for her. In order to motivate her to continue to excel, Grandmother prepared her favourite food, which was yam porridge. Habeebah ate the porridge with excitement. She was really motivated by Grandmother's incentive. She would continue to work hard in order to make her grandmother happy.

It seemed the experience that Habeebah's family had with the kidnapping had gradually faded. When school vacated, she resumed hawking. Grandmother couldn't help it. She had to feed her grandchildren. The only thing that changed was that they allowed the brightness of the morning to illuminate the earth before she set out on hawking.

Habeebah hawked throughout the holiday. She was able to make plenty of money for her grandmother. They ate good food and were happy. In the evening, she attended *madrasah* with her sibling and cousins. She coped well in *madrasah* because she was a brilliant girl.

She spent her holiday hawking and attending *madrasah*.

***

Khadijah spent her holiday in her house with her parents. Her parents made her holiday a memorable one by taking her out to different fun places. She went to the amusement park. She had fun and enjoyed herself. Her parents took her shopping. She bought shoes, clothes, toys and accessories. Her parents also took her to expensive eateries where she enjoyed cakes and pastries.

Her holiday was gradually coming to an end. There were just three days left. She had the most fulfilling holiday ever.

One morning, she woke up and used the toilet. When she wanted to flush, she realised the Water Closet had broken. The flush wasn't working again.

She went to the guest room to clean herself. Then after, she went to her mum's room to inform her about the faulty WC. Her mum called upon the maid to fetch water from another room to clean Khadijah's mess. Mrs. Oniru assured Khadijah that she would call the plumber to fix the broken WC.

Later that day, Mrs. Oniru and her husband had gone out to work. The maids were all downstairs. Khadijah was in her room upstairs. The plumber arrived and one of the maids brought him to Khadijah's room. The maid turned back and went downstairs after showing the plumber the faulty WC. The plumber started his work, while Khadijah was sitting on her bed, watching a documentary on her iPad.

Some minutes later, the plumber came out of the bathroom and informed Khadijah that he'd finished. He told her to check what he'd done. Khadijah got up from the bed and walked to the bathroom. She checked the WC flush and realised it was working again. She nodded her head in satisfaction. She was walking out of the bathroom when the plumber grabbed her hand.

She was shocked, she quickly snatched her hand from him and ran to the room. The plumber followed her immediately. He grabbed her hand again and drew her closer to him. Khadijah struggled to free herself but the plumber held her tightly.

"I'll give you chocolate," the plumber tried to cajole her.

"I don't want your chocolate. My parents gave me everything I ever wanted," Khadijah replied, while still struggling to release herself from the plumber's tight grip.

"I'll take you to Mr. Biggs," the plumber cajoled her again.

"I have been there so many times. Please, don't harm me, allow me to go," Khadijah pleaded in tears.

The plumber pushed her hard onto the bed. Khadijah tried to shout but the plumber covered her mouth.

While he was covering her mouth, Khadijah bit his palm so hard. The pain he felt made him unconsciously release his hold on her. She quickly ran out of the room. The plumber quickly got up and carried his tools.

Khadijah ran downstairs, while panting so heavily. He met two of the maids in the living room. They saw the way she was panting heavily. They asked her what was wrong but she couldn't speak.

At this time, the plumber had already gotten downstairs. Khadijah pointed at him. She was too traumatised to speak. Like someone who had a speech seizure, she couldn't say a word. She was just pointing at the plumber, while panting heavily. The plumber told the maids that he'd finished his work and he was leaving. Since Khadijah couldn't say anything but was only pointing, the maids couldn't decipher a thing.

The plumber walked hastily out of the house. This time, Khadijah's speech was restored. She shouted at the top of her voice.

"Please don't let him go. He tried to rape me," Khadijah suddenly shouted.

The plumber ran like a thief. All the maids ran after him. One of the maids was shouting for the gateman not to allow the plumber exit through the gate but the gateman could not hear. The plumber ran like a wind out of the gate, while the maids followed him. They were able to catch him on the next street. They took him back to Khadijah's house and beat him like the criminal that he was.

The maids put a call across to Khadijah's parents. They came running immediately. The plumber was handed over to the police.

Khadijah's mum hugged her tightly and comforted her. Khadijah's dad was fuming. He scolded the maids sternly.

"What am I paying all of you for? How can you leave my daughter alone in the room with an artisan? Are you all mad?!" Chief Oniru scolded his employees.

The employees said sorry countless times, but Chief Oniru continued to blast them and threatened them with sacking.

"A dog came to my house and molested my daughter under the watch of you useless people. So what am I paying you for if you cannot watch over my daughter while I'm away to work for the money I'll use in paying your salaries? You're all so useless. You're so worthless. You're good for nothing," Chief Oniru continued to burn with rage.

Khadijah's mum was just crying. She felt pity for her innocent daughter who was equally crying. Khadijah couldn't believe what just happened to her. She knew what rape was. Her parents had exposed her to many books and she'd learnt a lot. But she never knew she would have such a near experience. She cried bitterly. She couldn't stop crying. Her mum cried too and comforted her.

"I'm sorry, my darling daughter. I'm sorry I couldn't protect you from the pervert. I'm sorry you had to experience this. I'm so sorry, my darling. I hope he didn't have his way?" Mrs Oniru asked her daughter, who shook her head.

"No, mummy. But I was so scared. I thought he would harm me. I thought I wouldn't be able to escape," Khadijah cried.

"I'm sorry, my sweetheart. I'll never allow you to go through this experience again. I just thank God he didn't have his way. What would I have done? My only daughter! My precious daughter! My golden daughter! My pride! My joy! My forever motivation! I wake up everyday in search of greener pastures just because of you. I don't know what I'll do if anything happens to you. I'm so sorry for not being there when you needed me the most. I called the plumber to come over because I thought these useless maids would stay with him while working. But unfortunately, they left him alone to prey on my precious daughter. You're all fired! All of you! Pack your bags and get out of my house," Khadijah's mum retorted.

The maids begged to no avail. Khadijah's parents dismissed all of them for their irresponsibility.

Khadijah's mum was devastated. She was heart-broken. She blamed herself for not being there for her daughter. She blamed herself for not being able to protect her when she needed protection the most. She blamed herself for entrusting her responsibility to the maids. She blamed herself for negligence. She had always protected her daughter like a mother-hen. She took her to school everyday and picked her from school everyday, all by herself, without entrusting the duty to anyone, just so her daughter could be safe. She didn't allow her to attend *madrasah* outside the house. She hired a Quran teacher that would home-teach her instead, just so she could be protected from harm. But right there inside her house, the harm she'd been protecting her daughter from came to visit her.

Mrs. Oniru cried bitterly. Calamity had no identified customer. Calamity could strike anyone. No one is immune to calamity whether the poor or rich, calamity could visit anyone. Calamity visited Khadijah's family because of a simple carelessness. Mrs. Oniru cried and blamed herself that a single negligence on her part would have ruined her daughter's life.

Khadijah was traumatised because of the experience she had. She couldn't sleep at night. She always went to her parents' room to pass the night. She would wake up in the middle of her sleep and scream. Her parents had to take her to see a doctor. The general doctor advised them to see a psychologist. They booked an appointment with a psychologist. The psychologist worked together with a counselor who did lots of counselling sessions to revive Khadijah back to her old self. She told the psychologist that she always saw flashes of the incident whenever she was alone. The psychologist advised her parents never to allow her to stay alone for the time being.

Khadijah didn't resume with other students. She resumed a week after resumption. She was still going through a process of healing from the trauma.

CHAPTER ELEVEN

Khadijah resumed school a week after resumption. Even after she resumed, she was a bit withdrawn. She was snooty before and with the traumatic experience she suffered, she kept to herself even more. She became so touchy and irritable.

The second term started with serious academic activities. The students buckled down. The second term curriculum was more engaging compared to the first term. Teachers gave more practical work than they did during the first term.

Habeebah too was a little withdrawn this term. She had no problem from home other than the one she already had. But she missed Mrs. Babalola so much. She wished Mrs. Babalola was still in school with her. School life would have been more interesting. She missed her more because of the motherly advice she received from her, in addition with the money she usually gave her. Presently, she had to make do with the little her grandmother could afford.

She would take a bus to school so as not to be late in the morning. She spent just ₦10.00 during lunch break. Then she would trek home in the afternoon. She didn't allow all these challenges to affect her performance in school. She always remembered the advice of Mrs. Babalola not to allow her present challenges to blight her promising future. She worked harder everyday.

Khadijah was bouncing back gradually after lots of therapy sessions. She had started speaking to Aminah. Aminah was the only one she spoke to in class before. But since she experienced a rape attempt, she wouldn't speak to anyone in class, not even Aminah.

That day in class, Aminah was not getting her Mathematics tasks right. And to everyone's amazement, Khadijah got up from her seat and walked to Aminah's seat.

"Let me help you out," Khadijah offered to help Aminah.

"Oh, thank you so much," Aminah replied with smiles. "You don't know how much this means to me," Aminah said.

Khadijah collected Aminah's pen and explained the Mathematics topic to her. Meanwhile, Rasheed too was finding the topic difficult. When he noticed that Khadijah had helped Aminah, he quickly got up from his seat. By the time he could get to Aminah's seat, Khadijah was already through with Aminah and was returning to her seat. In a bid to call Khadijah's attention, Rasheed pulled her slightly by her arm. Khadijah turned back and upon realising that a boy's hand was touching her, she became ballistic and gave Rasheed a slap.

The whole class went into disarray. Rasheed wanted to retaliate the slap but Hamzah quickly held his hand.

"Leave my hand, let me slap this rude girl. How dare she slap me?" Rasheed lamented with rage, while Khadijah talked back at him sternly.

"How dare you touch me? The slap I gave you is little compared to what I'll do to you when next you touch me," Khadijah retorted, while Rasheed replied harshly, still struggling to give her a slap.

"What will you do to me when I next touch you?" Rasheed asked fiercely, charging at her.

"When next you touch me, I'll kill you," Khadijah replied daringly. The whole class exclaimed.

"Haaaaaaaaaaaaaa! Khadijah!!!!!!" The class exclaimed in surprise.

Rasheed was still trying to retaliate the slap Khadijah gave him. Hamzah held him tightly which prevented him from achieving his aim. The whole class was noisy. The noise attracted the teacher from the next class.

"Decorum!!!!" Mr. Ife shouted upon entering the JSS1A classroom.

The students, upon sighting him, ran to their various seats.

"What's happening here?" Mr. Ife demanded to know.

"Khadijah slapped Rasheed," Suwebah reported sharply.

"No, it was Rasheed that harassed Khadijah," Aminah quickly countered Suwebah.

The teacher was dazed at Aminah's information.

"Harass? What exactly did Rasheed do to Khadijah?" The teacher asked again.

"He didn't do anything to her?" Suwebah said again.

"No, he touched her," Aminah said again.

The teacher asked both Aminah and Suwebah to keep quiet.

"The two of you should keep quiet. Let me hear from the horse's mouth. Khadijah, what happened?" Mr. Ife asked Khadijah but instead of Khadijah to reply, she broke into tears to the amazement of the teacher.

"Why are you crying?" The teacher asked, surprised.

Khadijah couldn't reply, she continued weeping, non-stop.

The teacher turned to Rasheed.

"Rasheed, what happened between you and Khadijah?" Mr. Ife asked Rasheed.

"I wanted her to explain the topic we did in Mathematics today to me because I saw her doing the same for Aminah. I touched her in order to call her attention and she slapped me," Rasheed explained.

The teacher was surprised.

"Are you sure you only touched her and didn't do anything else?" Mr. Ife asked.

The other students except Aminah, Hamzah and Habeebah replied to the teacher.

"Yes, he only touched her. He didn't do anything else," the students chorused.

The teacher turned to the still-crying Khadijah.

He was forced to shout at her.

"Stop crying and tell me why you slapped your classmate when what he only did was touch you?" Mr. Ife shouted at Khadijah.

She didn't respond, she continued crying.

"She even said she'll kill Rasheed if he touches her again," Suwebah quickly added.

"Really? This type of attitude is not welcome at all," Mr. Ife scolded Khadijah.

Eventually, Mr. Ife took Khadijah to the principal's office because her behaviour seemed absurd to him. The principal too could not wrap her head around Khadijah's behaviour. Especially when she was told that Khadijah said she would kill Rasheed if he touched her again. To them, mere touching shouldn't warrant slapping her classmate. Little did they know that she was battling with trauma that arose from her past experience.

The principal told Khadijah to bring her parents to school the next day. If she failed to do so, she wouldn't be allowed into the school. Khadijah cried the whole of that day. She couldn't tell anyone what she was going through. Aminah came over to her seat and comforted her. She continued to cry until the close of school.

When her mum came to pick her, the first thing she noticed was Khadijah's swollen eyes. Mrs. Oniru became worried and asked Khadijah what the problem was. She couldn't respond. Her mum consoled her but she wouldn't stop crying.

When her dad returned in the evening, he also insisted on knowing what was wrong with her, but Khadijah didn't open up. After a lot of consoling and appealing, Khadijah eventually opened up to her parents. Her mum broke into tears. She cried for her helpless daughter who was still going through psychological trauma. She cried that her daughter was hurting badly and she couldn't do much to help her. Mrs. Oniru cried bitterly and asked her husband when Khadijah would be totally healed.

Chief Oniru had to act like a man. He bottled his own emotions in order to placate his wife and daughter. He consoled them not to cry anymore that Khadijah would soon get over the trauma and be completely healed. Chief Oniru comforted his wife and daughter soothingly. They ate dinner in a lighter mood and went to bed.

The following morning, the family woke up early. They got ready in no time. Khadijah's parents were following her to school to see the school principal. They got to school some minutes before assembly. They didn't allow Khadijah to attend the assembly. They waited patiently in their car until the assembly was over. The principal was a bit late that day. They waited patiently till she arrived.

The principal eventually arrived. Khadijah's parents allowed some minutes to pass before they went to her office. The office assistant told them to sit at the reception, while he went to inform the principal of their presence.

The assistant came back and ushered them into the principal's office. A discussion that lasted for a few minutes started.

The principal narrated what Khadijah did to her parents. They listened without interrupting her. After the principal was done, Khadijah's parents narrated the experience their daughter went through which made her so touchy. They told the principal that she was still in a process of healing after a series of therapy and counselling.

The principal was shocked at the revelation. She opened her mouth and couldn't close it.

She rushed to where Khadijah was sitting and embraced her.

"I'm very sorry, my sweetheart. I don't know that you've been through all this unpleasant experience. I'm so sorry for shouting at you yesterday. I'm sorry, in fact, I'll go to your class and tell your classmates never to touch you again. No one will touch you again, I'll make sure of that. I'm sorry, my angel. Don't worry, time will heal your wound. And please, don't brood too much over it. It wasn't your fault that what happened to you happened. You're a good girl and you'll excel in life," The principal motivated Khadijah.

The principal went to her class that very day to speak to her classmates. She told her classmates that Khadijah was a very good girl and she was only angry because Rasheed touched her instead of calling out her name. The principal scolded Rasheed that he shouldn't have touched her but just called out her name. The principal further warned the boys not to touch the girls in the class again and vise-versa.

"Verbal communication is better than gestures and touching," the principal told them.

The principal was able to settle the matter amicably and all grievances were put to rest. Khadijah was happy. She felt some warmth and affection by the principal's display of understanding. This gave her more confidence. It bolstered her sense of security. It rejuvenated her spirit. Her healing became faster.

***

The school was going on an excursion. The principal announced it at the assembly. The students were also given notes to take home to their parents. The school wanted to do something different that

academic session; so the students would be going to the Olumo Rock in Abeokuta for their excursion.

Each student was asked to pay ₦3000 for the trip which included transportation, gate fee and feeding. The students were excited. They'd been taught about rocks in the class. They'd seen photos of rocks in their textbooks, but none of them had seen a rock physically. They were anxious to go on the trip. They were eager to see and climb the rock.

All the students relayed the message to their parents. The next day in school, almost half of the school came with the excursion money.

Habeebah told her grandmother about the excursion. Grandmother replied without mincing words that she couldn't go for the excursion because there was no money. Habeebah grumbled out of her grandmother's presence. She decided to put a call through to her parents. She called her dad first. Her dad told her he wouldn't be able to raise ₦3000 at the moment as he'd been presently duped by fraudsters. She was disappointed. But she was still hopeful because she had the option of her mother.

Habeebah put a call through to her mother. She listened to how her mother lamented about low sales and the huge debt she'd incurred. Habeebah couldn't help but pity her mother. After being declined help by her parents, she cried bitterly. She really wished to go on the excursion. She wanted to see the much-talked-about Olumo Rock. She wanted to see how tall it was. She wanted to climb it to the top and scream in excitement. She wept bitterly, especially when it dawned on her that she might be the only one left out in her class.

That evening, her grandmother instructed her to make dinner. She was making dinner and crying profusely. Ade, one of grandmother's tenants, was passing by the kitchen and heard noises of weeping. He walked into the kitchen and saw that the noise was coming from Habeebah. He asked why she was crying. Habeebah continued crying without responding to Ade's question. Ade moved closer to her. He asked her why she was crying again.

"Please tell me why you're crying?" Ade insisted.

"It's nothing," Habeebah replied.

"How can you be crying for nothing?" Ade asked with utmost concern.

When Habeebah realised that his concern was genuine, she opened up to him.

"We're going on an excursion in school. Almost all my classmates have paid for the excursion but my grandmother, my father and my mother all said they don't have the money. I don't want to be the odd one out," Habeebah cried out.

Ade sighed before responding.

"How much are we talking about?" Ade asked.

"It's ₦3000. And we're going to Olumo Rock. I don't want to miss the trip. It's going to be so much fun and educational," Habeebah fantasised.

"Don't worry. You'll not miss the trip. I'll give you the money," Ade promised her.

Habeebah screamed excitedly.

"Are you sure?" Habeebah asked anxiously.

"I am very sure," Ade replied with a smug smile.

"It's ₦3000, *o*. Are you sure you can afford it?" Habeebah asked again in order to be sure.

"Yes, I can afford it. Don't you know I work? ₦3000 is nothing to me. In fact, it's chicken change," Ade boasted.

Habeebah smiled and showed him some gratitude.

"Thank you so much, brother Ade. I really appreciate your kindness. May God reward you abundantly. Please, when are you going to give me the money?" Habeebah asked eagerly.

"I'll give you this evening. Come to my room when you're done with your cooking," Ade said, Habeebah thanked him over and over again.

She hastened the cooking. She was done in no time. She informed her grandmother that she was done. Grandmother thanked her. She told her to serve her sibling and cousins. Habeebah quickly did as instructed. She did everything in haste. She doesn't want to miss the appointment with Ade.

After she was done with everything, she checked the corridor to be sure no one was watching her. After she was sure that it was safe for her, she walked stealthily towards Ade's room, while still checking her left and right. She got to Ade's door and knocked very gently. Ade asked who it was. Habeebah replied to him in a whisper. Ade got up to open the door for her.

Habeebah quickly walked in immediately after Ade opened the door. She was very conscious of her grandmother. She knew that her grandmother would scold her if she saw her walk into a boy's room.

Immediately after Habeebah entered Ade's room, she demanded for the money Ade promised her.

"I came to collect the money you promised me. Please give me the money before my grandmother finds out about my absence," Habeebah said with anxiety, while Ade smiled.

"Relax. I'll give you the money," Ade replied. He got up from the sofa he was sitting on and moved closer to the door.

He turned the key to a lock. Seeing this, Habeebah screamed. Ade quickly covered her mouth with his palm.

"Don't shout. You need money, don't you?"

"No, I don't need money again. Let me go please. Please allow me to go," Habeebah pleaded beneath Ade's palm.

"I cannot allow you to go. You want money, right? I have plenty of it. I'll give you everything you want," Ade said, while covering Habeebah's mouth with one hand and pushing her with the second hand.

"Please allow me to go. I don't want money again. Please don't harm me," Habeebah begged.

"I won't harm you. Why do you think I want to harm you? I just want you to give me something in exchange for the money I want to give you," Ade said, still covering Habeebah's mouth so tightly to prevent her from screaming.

"I don't want your money again. Please allow me to go," Habeebah pleaded and this time, a thought quickly ran through her head.

She bit Ade's hand very hard. The latter groaned in pain and impulsively released his hand from Habeebah's mouth. Habeebah pushed him away with all her might. She hurried to the door and unlocked it before Ade could get up. She ran out and didn't look back till she got to her grandmother's room.

Unknown to Habeebah, her grandmother was coming from the kitchen at the time she escaped from Ade's room. Grandmother saw her when she ran out of Ade's room.

Habeebah sat on the floor upon entering her grandmother's room and was panting heavily when grandmother walked in. She quickly composed herself. Grandmother stared sternly at her for a few seconds before speaking.

"I saw you ran out of Ade's room. What were you doing in Ade's room?" Grandmother asked impatiently.

"Nothing, *o*. I didn't...go to…...brother Ade's…… room ….to do anything," Habeebah stuttered.

"You didn't go there to do anything, right? So why did you run out of his room like a thief?" Grandmother shouted, losing her patience already.

"I...I...I....." Habeebah was stuttering when her grandmother gave her a hot slap.

She swiveled around like a barber's chair. Before she could get over the first slap, her cheek received a second slap from Grandmother. She cried out in pain.

"Start talking now before I cut your body with a razor and rub hot pepper on the cut," Grandmother threatened her sternly.

"I will talk," Habeebah cried out.

"Start talking now when I'm still nice. What were you doing in Ade's room?" Grandmother retorted.

"He.....He...He saw me crying in the kitchen. Then he asked why I was crying. I told him I needed ₦3000 for the school excursion. He said he would give me the money that I should come to his room. That was why I went to his room," Habeebah explained amidst tears.

Grandmother clapped her hands in dismay.

"You haven't finished the story. Why did you run out of Ade's room?" Grandmother shouted.

"He locked the door immediately after I walked into his room. He told me that I should give him something in exchange for the money he wanted to give me," Habeebah explained with misty eyes, while Grandmother's limb got weak immediately.

Grandmother sank weakly into the bed and clasped her hands on her head. She was speechless for minutes. She was too astonished to speak. When she found her voice, she spoke in tears.

"Habeebahhhhh! You really want to send me to my grave, don't you?" Grandma asked with teary eyes, while Habeebah shook her head.

"No, ma. I'm sorry for making you worry. I'm sorry, ma. I am very sorry," Habeebah repeated remorsefully.

"I told you I don't have money for the excursion your school is taking you on. You went ahead to beg from a man……," Grandmother was talking but Habeebah quickly interrupted her.

"I didn't beg from him. He was the one that offered to give me the money…..," she replied sharply amidst tears.

Grandmother shut her down.

"Keep quiet there! He offered to give you the money when you were crying. Why were you crying? Will you die if you don't go for the excursion? Had you not cried, he wouldn't have deceived you. He used your vulnerability against you. He used your helplessness against you. And that wouldn't have happened if you were content with what you have. That ₦3000 will feed us all for one week. Am I supposed to give that to you while we all starve?" Grandmother asked.

Habeebah shook her head.

"You see, my dear, in order to live a peaceful life, one must learn contentment. A content person is richly blessed. But an uncontented person will continue to pursue mirage until he meets his destruction. An uncontented person will steal in order to live a delusional life. An uncontented person will follow boys in order to live a luxurious life. There's no free lunch anywhere. What did I say?"

"There's no free lunch anywhere," Habeebah echoed with misty eyes.

"Yes, there's no free lunch anywhere. A boy will never give a girl something for free. He said he'll give you money and you believed him, did you work for him? He'll always expect something in return. If a girl dances to his tune and gives him what he's asking

for, her life will be ruined forever. Do you know what Ade is asking for?" Grandmother asked her.

"Yes, ma." Habeebah replied.

"What is he asking for?" Grandmother asked.

"He….He….wants….He….He wants to play with my body," Habeebah stuttered.

"Wow! I don't know that my granddaughter is this intelligent. Yes, you're right. But you're not entirely correct. He doesn't want to play with your body, he wants to sleep with you. That's the exchange he's talking about. Immediately he touches you like this, you'll become pregnant."

"Haaaaaaaaa!" Habeebah exclaimed.

"Yes, that is what will happen. That exchange will cost you your education. It will cost you your future. It will make your life redundant. While your mates are climbing the ladder of progress, you'll be descending the ladder retrogressively," Grandmother scared her, while she wept.

"I'll never do that again. I promise you that I'll never do that again."

"That's good. And I seriously hope you keep to your promise. Your body is very precious. You are the only one who has the right to touch your body. No one else has the right to touch it, whether a boy or girl, okay," Grandmother sounded a warning to her.

She nodded her head.

"Yes, ma." Habeebah replied.

"Good. You see, my darling, using what you have to get what you want as regards exchange of your body with material gifts is very destructive. That is why you should always be content with whatever you have. We'll not be in this condition forever. Things will still get better. There's still hope for a living person. It's not right to steal in order to keep up with your mates. It's not right to live a bad life in order to live up to your mates. You will not only go to Olumo Rock, by the grace of God, if you're patient, you'll also go to America, Saudi Arabia, London and so many other advanced countries," Grandmother prayed for Habeebah.

She replied with a resounding 'Aamin.'

"As for Ade, I am going to give him a notice of evacuation. He has to leave my house. He can't be molesting my granddaughter under my nose. How dare he?" Grandmother expressed angrily and quickly added, "I'll give you something that'll protect you from men," Grandmother said.

Habeebah thanked her with an affectionate hug.

CHAPTER TWELVE

On the day of the excursion, Habeebah didn't go to school. Her grandmother asked her to stay at home so that she wouldn't feel dejected when she saw her classmates going on the tour.

Around 8:10 that morning, her grandmother's phone rang. It was an unknown number. Grandmother picked it up and a voice greeted her from the other end of the phone.

"Hello, good morning. Am I on to Habeebah Adetola's grandmother?" The voice asked.

"Yes, you are. Who am I speaking with, please?" Grandmother responded.

"This is Mrs Davies, the principal of Kings and Queens College," the principal introduced herself, while Grandmother spoke with humility.

"Haaa, good morning, ma," Habeebah's grandmother responded humbly.

"I want to ask why Habeebah isn't in school today," the principal inquired.

"There's no problem at all. I can't afford to pay for the school excursion. And I see no reason for her to be in school today since she's not going for the excursion. I don't want her to feel dejected and left out," Grandmother explained.

"I perfectly understand. I don't know why she didn't come to me. I have told her to always come to me whenever she needs anything, Mrs. Babalola explained her situation to me before she left. I didn't know she didn't pay for the excursion not until the excursion supervisor was making a roll call and Habeebah was missing. Please send her to school now. I'll pay for her. Habeebah is a brilliant student. I can't allow her to miss this opportunity," the principal expressed.

Grandmother was too surprised to speak.

"Hello, ma. Are you still there?" The principal asked when Grandmother was silent.

"Yes, ma, I'm still here. Don't let us bother you, ma," Habeebah's grandmother rejected the principal's offer subtly.

"It is no bother at all. Please send her to school right away. The bus will take off any moment from now," the principal said with a tone of hastiness.

Habeebah's grandmother showered her with prayers.

"Thank you so much, ma. I am really grateful for this kindness. May God bless you and reward you abundantly. May your children find favour anywhere they go to. Thank you very much," Habeebah's grandmother prayed heartily.

"Aamin. You're most welcome, ma. I'll do anything for Habeebah over and over again. Please tell her to hurry," The principal said.

"She's coming right away. She's taken her bath. She'll just put on her school uniform and be on her way," grandmother said.

"Alright."

"Thank you so much."

"You're welcome," the principal replied and the call ended

***

The three buses that were conveying the students to Olumo Rock in Abeokuta were on stand-still till Habeebah arrived. Immediately after Habeebah arrived, the buses moved.

They travelled for one hour and some minutes from Lagos to Abeokuta where the Olumo Rock was situated.

The road trip was fun. The students were very anxious to see the rock. Some of them had goosebumps on their body. An indescribable excitement was oozing out of them. They couldn't wait to climb the rock to the top and scream their lungs out.

A teacher was saddled with the responsibility of telling the students the names of places as they journeyed. Anytime they reached a landmark, Mr. Akorede would make some explanations regarding the history of the particular landmark. The students had fun. Mr Akorede told them an excursion is learning outside the four walls of a classroom. And the students indeed learnt a lot.

They were told the names of bus-stops as they led to one another. The students also asked questions. The teacher never got tired of answering their questions. The question and answer learning-process made their journey stress free and short. They didn't realise they'd gotten to Abeokuta until the driver drove into the monument gate and pulled the vehicle to a stop.

They alighted from the bus after they'd reached their destination. The excursion supervisor paid for the gate fee. A tour guide was already on standby to guide them through.

The students were shown around the ancient rock by a tour guide. It was a sight to behold! The students were told stories about the origin of the rock. The tale of the rock was an exciting one to listen to. The tour guide was quite knowledgeable about the historical landmark. He had a sense of humour too. The students laughed as he passed some jokes, while dishing the history of the Egba people to them.

According to the tour guide, Olumo was actually derived from "*Oluwa Lomo*" meaning, "God benevolently molded this rock for our refuge." [2]

In the 19th Century, Olumo Rock served as a rock fortress for the people of Egbaland where it housed the *Egba* warriors for 3 years.

The younger students were made to use the stairs instead of climbing the rock, while the older students and the teachers climbed the rock. The climbing was so much fun. And also a form of exercise.

The view from the top was so exhilarating. The blue sky seemed nearer on the mountain top, while the earth seemed farer with tiny views.

The beauty of nature from the mountain top was captivating. The sight on the mountain top captured the sky and earth vividly.

After spending some exciting time on the mountain, the students were guided back to the last floor.

They visited the gallery next. They saw beautiful pieces of paintings, ancient beads, sculptors, etc. Some of the teachers bought paintings. Some students who had extra money also bought paintings and ancient beads.

By the time they left the gallery, it was time for lunch. The students were served a nice meal. White amala, also known as *lafun*, was the delicacy. A visit to *Egba* would not be complete without the consumption of their food; *lafun*.

The teachers were also served.

After the meal, the students were asked to rest, while some of the teachers visited the *Adire* shops. Apart from the historical landmark of Olumo Rock, Abeokuta is also known for *Adire* fabrics. A trip to Abeokuta would also not be complete without visiting the *Adire* shops too.

Some of the teachers bought nice *Adire* fabrics. Some students whose parents gave plenty of extra money also bought *Adire* fabrics.

The experience was a once in a lifetime one. The students took down some notes, while the tour guide was giving background into the history of the rock and city earlier. Their teachers told them there would be questions concerning the trip in their forthcoming examination.

The students and their teachers left the city of Abeokuta at exactly 3.00 p.m to make a return journey to Lagos. The return journey was tiring compared to the arrival journey. The students were tired. Most of them slept throughout the journey.

They got to Lagos some minutes before 5.00 p.m. Parents and guardians were already awaiting their arrival. The buses entered the school gate. Students alighted into the waiting arms of their parents. Words of gratitude filled the air. To go on a journey and return safely was worth glorifying God for.

The second term exam came and indeed, there were questions concerning the excursion. It came out in the English essay, titled: MY TRIP TO OLUMO ROCK.

The students performed excellently. As the saying goes, 'What I hear I forget. What I see I remember.' None of the students forgot the experience and they were able to relay it in the essay.

The second term ended with Khadijah Oniru topping the class with first position, while Habeebah had the second position and Hamzah, the third position. Anat Omotosho came behind Hamzah with the fourth position.

Khadijah, as usual, gallantly walked to her mother's car. She garrulously narrated how she came first again to her mother. Her mother congratulated her. Mrs. Oniru watched her daughter in admiration as she talked non-stop till they reached the house. A special delicacy was prepared for her as usual. Her parents were excited that the experience she had, never dwindled her performance in school.

Habeebah Adetola's grandmother was excited about her position. Grandmother was proud of her. She promised to buy a new school shoe for her by next term.

***

During the holiday, Khadijah Oniru became more inquisitive. It seemed her psychological puberty had started because she became more mentally alert. She became more sensible and asked a lot of questions.

During the holiday, her mother taught her sex education. The woman had to because her daughter would not stop asking questions.

"The first step of sex education is awareness of your body parts which I'm sure you are already familiar with, especially your private areas, is that not so?" Mrs. Oniru asked her daughter.

"Yes, mummy," Khadijah replied.

Her mother elaborated better.

"The vagina and penis are a girl and a boy's private areas. You must know that these areas are your private areas which belong to only you and can be touched by only you, mummy or daddy when they're cleaning for you. After you're old enough to clean yourself up, these private areas shouldn't be touched by anyone else. Unnecessary personal touching is frowned at. You can only touch your private areas when necessary. Private areas are not toys that you can play with. Unnecessary touching of the private areas can arouse excitement and pleasure. In advanced term, it is called masturbation. This is dangerous because it can cause addiction. When children are addicted to touching their private areas, their sexuality grows widely and this can lead to more dangerous occurrences," Mrs. Oniru educated her daughter.

Khadijah nodded her head.

Her mother continued.

"Identifying the difference between you and a boy is important. For example, you have body parts which are different from that of a boy; like the breast and vagina. You must understand that the coming together of these different body parts can arouse excitement and pleasure, this is why these two distinct body parts should be kept away from each other. Hugging should be avoided. By hugging, your breast is resting on the chest of a boy, this can stimulate pleasure. Then above all, the private area of the girl must not come in contact with the private area of the boy until a legal marriage is done. The illegitimate coming together of the two private areas is a sin and will result in pregnancy."

"Haaa!!!!" Khadijah exclaimed.

"Why are you exclaiming? Didn't I mention this when I taught you puberty?"

"You did," Khadijah replied.

"Very good. Touching of any kind should be avoided; handshake, hugging, sitting together and every other form of skinship. Unnecessary and unguarded body contacts with the opposite sex can lead to the coming together of the two private areas. You should avoid it, is that clear?"

"Yes, mummy. Thank you, mummy."

"You're welcome. This will be a continuous admonition henceforth. I will never shy away from teaching you sex education," Mrs Oniru made a determination.

Khadijah nodded her head and thanked her mother.

CHAPTER THIRTEEN

The school resumed for the third term academic session after three weeks of holiday.

Khadijah Oniru felt more confident because of the knowledge she just acquired from her mother. When school resumed, she narrated everything to Aminah, her friend. Aminah told her that her mother had given her sex education too.

"My mother told me that her mother never gave her sex education. And so she made a decision not to make me go through the ignorance she went through. She enlightened me about a lot of things," Aminah Badmus told Khadijah.

"Really! That's very impressive. I don't think my mother would have told me anything if I didn't ask her questions," Khadijah Oniru stated.

"Well, maybe. My mother told me that sex education is a topic mothers do shy away from. But she made an intentional decision not to make me lack it the way she lacked it while growing up," Aminah said.

"Really! Please tell me, what are the things your mother told you?" Khadijah was curious.

"Everything your mother told you. Except that my mother added things like, 'don't sit on a man's lap when you find yourself inside a public bus. She told me she personally had a bitter experience concerning that," Aminah said.

"Really! Can you share it with me?" Khadijah urged.

"Sure. My mother told me that when she was a little girl of seven, her mother took her out and they boarded a commercial vehicle. She told me that particular commercial vehicle was called *MOLUE* back then in Lagos. It's just like the Bus Rapid Transit: BRT bus we use in Lagos today but the difference is that *MOLUE* was not sophisticated. It used to be so rowdy. That particular day, my mother told me that when she entered the vehicle with her mother, the seats had all been occupied. They both had to stand. A male co-passenger who noticed how unbearable standing was, for a little girl, especially when she wasn't tall enough to hold on to the strap for balance, offered to carry my mother on his lap. My grandmother agreed. She thought it would be a relief for her daughter. The man carried my mother on his lap and as they journeyed, he began to thrust my mother's buttocks with his penis. My mother said she was uncomfortable but she couldn't understand what was going on. The man did that till he discharged some fluid on my mother's gown. After they got down from the vehicle, her mother noticed her wet gown and asked what was wrong, she couldn't explain. The memory of that day still lingers in her head. My mother vowed never to make me go through what she went through. She always protects me like an egg. She also equipped me with everything I need to protect myself; like knowledge," Aminah narrated her mother's experience.

"That was really horrible. Please tell me the other things your mum told you," Khadijah pleaded. She was enjoying the discussion.

"She also told me that no man is allowed to call me 'my wife', and so many other things. My mother never joked with that of older men calling little girls 'my wife.' We once had a driver who used to playfully address me as his wife, but my parents sacked him without a second thought," Aminah said, while Khadijah shrugged.

"Is calling a girl 'my wife' not a joke?" Khadijah asked.

"No, my mum said it's not a joke and it shouldn't be taken as a joke, especially when peadophiles abound in the society," Aminah explained.

"Peadophile? What's that?" Khadijah wanted to know.

"My mum said that a peadophile is an adult who is sexually attracted to, or engages in sexual acts with a child. My mum narrated a story that happened in her neighbourhood while she was growing up. A young man used to live in the same compound with a woman and her little daughter. The man used to call the little girl of age five his wife," Aminah narrated.

"Hmmmmm," Khadijah sighed.

"The mother thought it was an innocent joke just like you think now. Anytime the girl's mother passed by the man with the girl, the man would play with the girl's cheek and call her his wife. He would also give the little girl biscuits and chocolate. The mother became relaxed and trusted the man to love her daughter genuinely. Whenever the woman was going out, he would leave the girl with the man. Little did she know that the man was molesting the little girl. It was too late by the time she found out. The neighbours beat the man like a thief but the beating cannot undo the damage he'd done to the girl. The best thing is to protect your kids from harm. Don't trust strangers with your children. Don't entrust your children with strangers. Especially young kids that can't report if any harm comes their way. Nobody should be trusted. A mother should be very vigilant and protective like the mother-hen. That's what my mother said," Aminah reported sagely.

Khadijah heaved before responding.

"Your mother is very right," Khadijah remarked and looked around to ensure no one was listening to their conversation before speaking in a whisper.

"Did you know I had a similar experience?" Khadijah said in a whisper.

Aminah gasped.

"*Subhana'llah*!" Aminah exclaimed.

"Thank God he didn't have his way. He was an artisan who came to repair our broken WC. My mum entrusted me to the maids. She thought a maid would stay with the plumber while he worked but none of the maids did. The plumber wanted to rape me. I was so scared. Allah saved me but the trauma haunted me for months. I became very touchy. Do you remember the day I slapped Rasheed when he touched me?"

"Yes I do."

"I was still having the replay of the incident in my head. Any touch, be it innocent or harmful would always arouse my anger. *Alhamdulillah*, now I am better with consistent therapy. I quite agree with your mum that no one should be trusted. A mother should protect her child like a mother-hen, indeed."

"I am so sorry about your experience. I'm glad you're better. My mother will always preach it like a gospel, 'don't allow older men to call your daughters 'my wife' 'Never entrust your child with a stranger' 'Be observant enough to know if your daughter is not comfortable with a particular adult' My mother would say that a mother should be a psychologist who can read both the minds and gestures of her children," Aminah added.

"That's very true. I'll make sure I instill the necessary values in my children and protect them from harm. Thank you Aminah for teaching me a new word today," Khadijah appreciated her friend.

"What's that?" Aminah asked.

"Peadophile," Khadijah responded.

Aminah smiled.

"You're welcome."

The two girls continued with their discussion till a teacher walked into the class.

***

The term raced like a horse. The teachers also raced to cover all the topics before exams. The JSS1A students were fully prepared for exams. The teachers did revisions with them before exams.

The JSS1 students looked forward to the terminal JSS1 exams. They couldn't wait to be promoted to JSS2.

They studied hard for the exams. The principal had admonished them several times on the importance of studying hard. "He who fails to prepare would prepare to fail," the principal told them.

The third term exam was done with and the students only came to school to bond with their friends, while their teachers prepared their report cards.

On one of such days of bonding, the students of JSS1A were in the classroom when Abbas brought a game suggestion. 'Name, Name, Name' was the name of the game.

"Who's in?" Abbas asked, while interested people raised their hands.

Abbas explained the rules of the game to his mates. The game required the participants to mention names of places, colours, countries, phones, names of people, animals, etc.

Most of the girls were not interested in participating except Suwebah and Adebisi. Almost all the boys were interested.

Abbas arranged the participants in an orderly version and each person will come after another.

Abbas started with the preamble, Name Name, Name, name of animals, name of animals:

Abbas: Jaguar
Hamzah: Hippopotamus
Adebisi: Lion
Rasheed: Camel
Akande: Cheetah
Titi: Tiger

Kamil: Deer
Saheed: Leopard
Shina: Dog
Jide: Donkey
Chinedu: Horse
Suwebah: Elephant
Ajike: Jaguar

"I have already mentioned Jaguar. Ajike, you're disqualified," Abbas said.

Ajike was disqualified and they started with another topic.

"Name, Name, Name, name of countries, name of countries:

Abbas: America.
Hamzah: Hungary
Adebisi: Argentina
Rasheed: Rwanda
Akande: Africa

Akande goofed and the whole class burst into a sarcastic laughter. When the laughter subsided, Rasheed spoke.

"Akande! Africa is not a country but a continent," Rasheed corrected him.

Akande hissed and left the game as he'd been disqualified according to Abbas' rules. The rest of the participants continued.

It was Titi's turn.

Titi: Turkey," Titi said, while Abbas cut in sharply.

"Turkey *ko*, Titus *ni*. Why don't you tell us that you want to eat Turkey?......" Abbas was speaking ignorantly, but Hamzah interrupted him.

"Even you Abbas ain't qualified for this game because you're an ignoramus. You mean you don't know that Turkey is a country?" Hamzah asked, rather surprised.

"How can Turkey be a country, isn't Turkey an animal, the one we eat?" Abbas asked ignorantly.

Khadijah, who wasn't part of the game but only an observer replied to him.

"Turkey is the name of a country. My dad told me that the word 'Turkey' has meant 'the land of the Turks' since ancient times. Turkey is partly Asia and partly Europe. Turkey is also an animal, a white bird. And yes, the one that we eat. Do you now understand, Abbas?" Khadijah explained brilliantly and concluded it with a question.

"Thank you, Khadijah. Now I understand," Abbas expressed and then added: "Let's continue the game.

The other participants continued the game.

Kamil: Korea

Saheed: Senegal

Shina: Saudi Arabia

Jide: Japan

Chinedu: Cameroon

Suwebah: Brazil.

"Suwebah, you're disqualified." Abbas said sharply, while Suwebah flared up.

"Is Brazil not the name of a country?" Suwebah asked angrily.

"Yes, it is. But didn't you notice the trend?" Abbas asked her.

"What's the trend?" Suwebah asked him with a hard stare.

"The trend is that we've all been providing a name of the country that starts with the first letter of our names," Abbas replied to Suwebah.

Suwebah hissed.

"No way. I'll never accept that. When you were stating the rules, that wasn't part of the rules that you stated," Suwebah protested.

Hamzah seconded her.

"Suwebah is right. Abbas, you didn't include rhyme in the rules you stated; so, Suwebah isn't disqualified," Hamzah said.

"Okay, okay. I accepted that I didn't include rhyme in the rules. But now I want to include it. The name you provide now must start with the first letter of your name. It will be more fun that way. Let's go! Name, name, name, name of phones, name of phones.

Abbas: Alcatel

Hamzah: Huawei

Adebisi: Acer

Rasheed: ....

"Rasheed, you're disqualified," Abbas said, while Rasheed grumbled.

"I'll never accept that. Is there a phone name that starts with the letter R?" Rasheed protested.

"I don't know, *o*. If you think very well, there should be one. And if there's none, that's your own luck," Abbas replied mockingly.

Rasheed hissed and left the game.

The rest of the participants continued.

Titi: Techno

Kamil: ....

Kamil couldn't provide the name of a phone that started with the first letter of his name. So he was disqualified. The others continued.

Saheed: Samsung

Shina: Sendo

Jide: ....

Jide was lost, so he was disqualified.

Chinedu: Casio

Suwebah: Nokia.

Suwebah said, while the class laughed.

"Suwebah, you're disqualified. Does Nokia start with the letter S?"
Abbas asked her. Suwebah challenged him to name a phone that
started with the letter S apart from Samsung and Sendo which
Saheed and Shina had earlier mentioned. Abbas blabbered.
Suwebah hissed at him.
"Can you see? If it's that easy, why can't you provide an answer?"
Suwebah challenged Abbas.
"Don't hiss at me, *o*. Is it my fault? Maybe you should change your
name to Aisha. There are lots of phones that start with the letter
A," Abbas teased her.
Suwebah rolled her eyes at him. And Rasheed defended Suwebah
to pay back Abbas' tauntings.
All along, the game was fun but it ended with a fight. The students
went home early because there was no serious activity in school.
The following day was vacation day where students would collect
their report cards.

***

The following day, the school vacated for the end of the third term
which also marked the end of the session.
The students rolled in to collect their report cards. Khadijah Oniru
jumped up happily after topping the class with the first position
again. She was able to cling on to the first position for the whole of
the three terms in the session. She ran joyously to break the news
of her outstanding success to her mother when she came to pick
her home.
Habeebah Adetola maintained the second position without
faltering. She was delighted. Her struggles through hot and cold
didn't debar her from excelling. Her grandmother was ever proud
of her.
Hamzah Bello came next to Habeebah with the third position. He
was happy. His intention was never to compete but to excel. And

his overall percentage was impressive. There was just a little difference between the percentage of the first and second position. The margins were tiny which showed that the trio of Khadijah, Habeebah and Hamzah performed exceptionally. It was most likely that their class teacher had a tough call in deciding their positions. All the students were promoted to JSS2. They all looked forward to their new class eagerly.

GLOSSARY

Adhan: The islamic call to prayer, recited by a muadhin at prescribed times of the day.

Rakat: The name used for the series of movements performed during Salat prayer.

Muadhin: The person who issues the call to prayer from one of the minarets of a mosque.

Rakatain fajr: Two rak'ahs sunnah prayer before Fajr Salah

Iqamah: The Islamic second call to salah (prayer).

Salat or Salah: The Arabic word for the five daily prayers enjoined on Muslims by Allah.

Subh: One of the five mandatory salah, precisely the 1st prayer of the day.

Maghrib: One of the five mandatory salah, precisely the 4th prayer of the day.

Ishai: One of the five mandatory salah, precisely the 5th prayer of the day.

Madrasah: The Arabic word for any type of educational institution, secular or religious, especially a school where Islamic knowledge is learnt.

Hadith: What the majority of Muslims believe to be a record of the words, actions, and silent approval of the Islamic Prophet Muhammad.

Seerah: The study of the life of the Prophet Muhammad.

Sahabiyyah: Female companions of the prophet

Kaffir: An arabic term which refers to a person who disbelieves in God as per Islam or denies his authority, or rejects the tenets of Islam.

Ekaaro ologi de: Good morning to everyone, the pap seller is around.

Alhamdulillah: Glory be to Allah

SubhanAllah: Praise be to Allah

Adhkar: Words or phrases of remembrance of Allah.

Fiqh: The theory or philosophy of Islamic law, based on the teachings of the Quran and the traditions of the Prophet.

Adire: Meaning, "tie and dye" commonly worn by the Egba people of Ogun State.

Egba: A Yoruba-speaking people of southwestern Nigeria primarily concentrated in the vicinity of Abeokuta.

REFERENCES

Quran

Hadith

The English dictionary

Citadel of the believer

Short stories of sahabiyat by Samina. Published by http://ayeina.com

CLOSE CALL is the story of peer pressure. Habeebah Adetola's vulnerability sold her out to peer pressure. She desires a good life but she takes the wrong path. She has a close call with destruction and death before she is saved by the whisker. The story also talks about menstruation and menstrual hygiene for high school students. Interesting school activities are also featured like debate, seerah, plays and teasers among others.

TEEN ADVENTURE is a story that borders around our teenagers' escapades with smartphones and social media. Suddenly, the world was afflicted with CoronaVirus and the majority of our high school students have access to smartphones all of a sudden to participate in school online classes. The ecstasy, the enthusiasm and excitement introduced them to another world entirely. Book three explores the dangers of smartphones and social media for high school students.

It talks about child abuse and its various forms. It also features fascinating school activities like debate, seerah, plays and teasers among others.

THE NEW BOY introduces Adam Akintola, the Ibadan boy, into the story. Adam didn't start Kings and Queens College from JSS1 like the rest. He joined the school in SS1 and his grand entrance made a twist to the story. He gave Khadijah Oniru a run for her brain. This resulted in rivalry, contempt and verbal abuse. The story also features enthralling school activities, like debate, seerah, plays and teasers, like the rest.

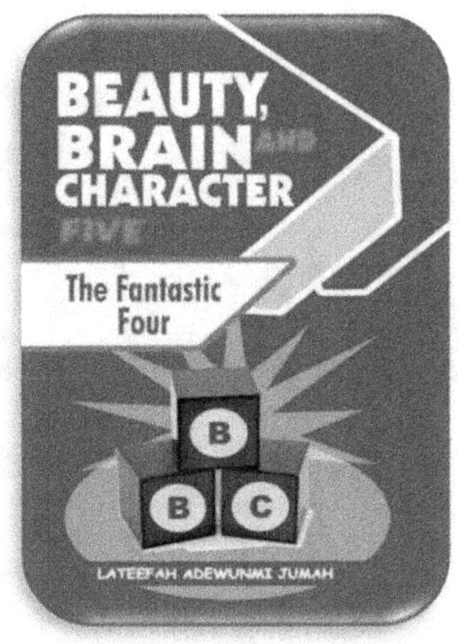

THE FANTASTIC FOUR explores the activities of Adam, Khadijah, Hamzah and Habeebah as they take over the mantle of the leadership of Kings and Queens College through their brilliant brains. They become the faces of the school's competition and they win several prizes for the school.

The story also features intriguing school activities like debate, seerah, plays, excursion, teasers and Islamic sex education and so on.

LIFE AFTER HIGH SCHOOL begins with SS3 activities and later explores the after school life of the casts. The higher institution they went to, their career, marriage and the likes. Book six is the summary of all the other five. It's appropriate for SS3 students and adults. It features engaging school activities like debate, seerah, play, teasers, excursion, Islamic sex education and so on. It also spots general life lessons.